The Summer That Dried My Tears

Casey L Brown

Thanks to all of my friends and family for your support on this endeavor. Special thanks to my mother and husband for their countless hours of holding my hand on this journey.

Contents

Chapter 1

Whoosh! A cool gust of wind blew in through the open city bus window, as I watched a gaudy, bright yellow car fly past. I peered out the window and up at the sky, which was a dismal gray with a smattering of ominous clouds. The bus made a few more stops until it came to a sad looking, beat-up, green bench, which was still four blocks from the apartment I shared with my father.

The bus's worn brakes slowed it to a halt and I lugged my backpack and purse off the bus, dumping them onto the green bench. I watched fondly as the bus sped away. *Next stop, my apartment.* Groaning a little as I snatched up my bags, I began my journey home. Reading is my one joy in this world, my only escape, and my poor, distressed backpack revealed years of being stuffed with books. I grabbed my purse as well, which had its own lot of sugar packets from the pizza place I worked at, for my cheap dad to put in his coffee.

There are days when my walk is worth it, considering I get to pass through a park with a gorgeous water fountain in the center, along with numerous flowering bushes. I have always enjoyed the peace and serenity of the place. This day, however, I was not lucky enough to be able to spend much time in the park. I had to get home to talk to my dad. The annual Teen's Night Out was coming up in just a few days at our local bar and ballroom, and I was praying he would let me go. It would be the perfect start to the summer after just finishing high school and although Bill, my father, has never let me go before, I had hope now that I was 18 years old.

Finally, I reached our building and pushed through the double glass doors. Connected to the lobby is a little coffee shop where my best friend, Henna, worked. I walked up to a counter with a service window and saw her in the shop. I gave her a smile. She returned the gesture with a wink. Henna handed me a small cup of decaf hazelnut, the color of Henna's hair, sweetened just the way I like it, and I handed her a few dollars and said thanks. As I turned to head to the elevator, she leaned out and tapped my shoulder and in a hushed voice she asked,

"Hey, Danny, are you going to TNO? 'Cause everyone we know is gonna be there. It'd be a shame if you missed it...again." Henna rolled her eyes.

"Henna, you know how Bill is." I glanced down at my worn-out sneakers. "He doesn't trust me, not to mention the *boys* that'll be there. He barely lets me outta the house other than school and work, and I think I'm lucky I even get that."

"I know, but I hope you can convince him." She gave me a pleading, yet sympathetic look. "Besides, if you talk to him now, he'll be sober. It's still pretty early in the evening." She seemed hopeful.

"Yeah, sure. I gotta go before he gets pissed at me for being late." I glanced back up at her. "See ya later," I mumbled, trying to put a convincing smile on my face.

I walked over to the elevator and pushed the button. The doors creaked open and I stepped in. I used the ride up to the fourth floor to gather my thoughts. How I dreaded having to bring this up to my dad. Maybe dread wasn't the right word, more like I was terrified to bring it up to my dad. The elevator jerked to a stop and let me out. I sauntered down the hall. *How would I even start this conversation?* My dad wasn't exactly normal. When my mother was still alive, they would fight all the time, sometimes with more than just words. The police were called on him more than once. He's a dangerous man with a short temper. Dealing with him is a fine art, like dodging bullets or walking on a minefield, made especially difficult if he is drunk, which is typical any time after 4 o'clock.

My throat clenched, and I could feel the sweat on my neck as I reached out for the door handle. I closed my eyes and took a breath, then pushed the door open. Bill was sitting in his recliner smoking a cigarette. I chose my words carefully.

"Hey, Dad," I said tentatively. "I was just talkin' to Henna and..." I couldn't get the question out. "I got a coffee. Would you like a sip?" I sputtered out.

"No," he replied coldly. He didn't even bother to look back at me. "There're dishes to be done, so don't just stand around," He announced harshly, and I got the feeling that he intended I do them now. Letting out a breath, I took off my shoes and walked into the kitchen. The cool tiles felt nice on my hot feet. Dumping my stuff on the small kitchen table, I glanced at the pile of dishes. Sipping on my coffee, I walked over to stand on the soft kitchen mat by the sink and turned on the water. Setting the coffee down on the counter, I grabbed the lavender scented dish soap. It smelled lovely as I poured some into the basin. The sound of the water relaxed my tense mood a bit. Bill continued to watch some kind of college sports. I started with the glasses. The action and warm water were soothing. I was so entranced with the dishes after a while that I jumped a little when my father spoke, and I almost dropped his favorite beer glass.

"Danny, I've seen the posters up for that teen party thing coming up," he said coolly. "You remember my rules?"

"Well, actually, I wanted to speak with you about that," I answered.

"You're not going. It's at a bar and there will be boys. I know boys and what they think, and they don't need to be thinking about my girl that way. I won't have it," he said firmly. I looked down at the dish water and decided I'd try and push my luck tonight. He has never let me do anything. Maybe just this once he'd bend. I gathered my voice.

"Dad, I could go with Henna. She's been my friend for years and wouldn't let anything happen to me. I'll steer clear of the guys, trust me. I just wanna go have fun with my friends. If you want, I'd even check in with you on my phone. Just please, I really—"

He cut me off. "No! You won't be attending! Don't try to push the issue!"

I had been staring down into the dishes so hard, I hadn't heard him come up behind me. When he grabbed my shoulder, shock pulsed through me. I let out a yelp. Knowing it would only make things worse, I didn't try to struggle away from him. He grabbed both of my hands, one of which held a small paring knife. He squeezed them tightly and I could feel the blade pierce into my palm. I stifled another cry as silent tears streaked down my face. I gritted my teeth. He must've finally realized what he was doing and let my hands go, shoving me away from him. I slammed against the edge of the sink and held onto it, shaking while he stalked back into the living room, grumbling. I listened for the sound of him dropping back into his chair as if nothing had happened. My hand was throbbing as I looked down at it. I watched as the brilliant, red blood oozed out of the gash on my palm. Gritting my teeth, I turned on the water and felt the sting as I let it wash some of the blood away. I grabbed the dish towel and applied it to my palm as I headed for my bathroom.

I went into the tiny room. Turning on the lights with my nose, I shut the door with my elbow. Hunching over the small pedestal sink, I nudged on the cold water and stuck my palm into the stream. I watched as the water was stained with my blood. I looked up at the mirrored medicine cabinet, careful not to make eye contact with the black haired, fair skinned girl in the mirror. I didn't want to see her like this. Yanking the door of the cabinet open, I searched for the medical kit. Finding it, I picked out a wad of gauze and some thick, sticky medical tape. Shutting off the water, I patted the cut dry with the stained dish towel and quickly applied the medical gauze and snugly secured it with the tape. I shut the cabinet door and looked in the mirror. This time I made eye contact with her and watched as her hazel eyes filled with tears. The person looking back at me held a gut wrenchingly pained expression.

Looking away from her, I backed up and sat down on the edge of the porcelain bathtub pondering how many more times I would have to dress a wound or put makeup on a black eye. I looked down at my bandage deciding I would have Henna look at the cut tomorrow. Her father was a doctor and she had learned a lot from him over the years. She was planning on studying to become a nurse.

Wiping my tears with the back of my hand, I strode out into the hall, directly into my tiny bedroom, and shut the door. Not bothering to turn on the lights, I sat down on my bed. I stared at the barely visible blue walls and made a silent vow to myself that I would not let this happen to me again... somehow.

Chapter 2

*O*uch! My hand stung as I smacked it down on my blaring alarm clock. After shaking it off, I got up and opened my closet, pulled out clothes for work, and went to the bathroom. I flicked on the lights and locked the bathroom door. The bright light made me squint for a moment. Grabbing my hairbrush out of the cabinet, I dragged it through my tangled, glossy black hair. Next, I dusted some powder on my fair skin and used just a little blush on the apples of my cheeks. Lastly, I did a sweep of mascara on my lashes, so I would look more alive.

I finished getting dressed and walked down the short hall leading to the kitchen. I had hoped that my dad was either asleep or out getting something. I was ready to sneak past his room when I heard the TV blaring in the living room. It's okay, if he says something, I'll just have to be on my toes. I reached the kitchen and grabbed yesterday's stale coffee. Quickly, I chugged it down, then grabbed my purse from the table. I turned and went towards the door. As I was reaching for the handle, my dad spoke.

"When you leave work today, pick me up a pack of cigarettes. And don't goof around. Get back here with that as soon as you can." The whole time he was talking, I never turned to look at him. I just kept my eyes locked on the door handle.

"Okay, I will." I opened the door and left.

Once in the hallway, I was able to finally breathe again. I scrambled to the elevator. I wanted to get away from that man. During the summer, work was the only way for me to get out of the house and I was thankful for it. If I didn't work, I'd basically be my dad's prisoner. A princess locked away in a tower.

When I reached the ground floor, I practically dove through the doors onto the tile floor. I went straight outside, thankful to be free, if only for a little while. I didn't have a car, so I headed for the bus stop. I walked past all of the neighboring apartments and businesses. I got to the beautiful park and took a moment to enjoy the fountain and the rose buds. Not wanting to be late, I hoofed it to the bus stop and boarded in perfect time. I took the closest empty seat and stared out the window. It wasn't a very long ride. The city wasn't huge. I hopped off the bus steps at my stop and crossed the street to the pizza parlor. Popping through the doors, I skipped behind the counter to punch in. Jason, the manager, was behind the counter. He and I went to school together, so it gets kind of awkward between us, but at least he is kind. I have always thought he likes me too, but I'm not particularly interested in him. Not that he wasn't good looking, with a lean build, brown hair, and pretty blue eyes. However, if I had a boyfriend and my father found out, he would freak. I walked up to Jason.

"Hey, Jason, what do you need me to do this morning?" He turned to me.

"Not much yet today. Just start with wiping off the tables." With a polite smile, I nodded and snatched a spray bottle and towel out of the cleaning supplies. I strode into the dining area and started by taking the chairs down off of the tables. Then, I sprayed one and began wiping off any missed spots from yesterday's last customers. I was also sure to wipe down the seats, so they glistened in the dim lighting. It seemed like I had been working for a while, so I checked around the room for customers and then peeked at the clock on the wall, only to find out that it still wasn't even close to opening. Finishing with the tables, I went back behind the counter to find out what my next task would be. I found Jason turning on appliances and wiping down counters. It was still early and none of the other workers had arrived yet. Walking over to Jason, I gently took the towel away from him and proceeded to wash the counters myself, freeing him up for more important work. He smiled at me.

We worked in silence for a while doing monotonous tasks and getting the kitchen ready. Jason broke the silence.

"Danica?" he asked tentatively. "Are you going to Teen's Night Out with anyone?"

"No," I replied suspiciously. Then I figured out what he might be getting at. *Was he asking me to go with him?* He must have figured that was all I had to say, so he continued.

"I was just wondering 'cause I'm going with a group of friends. Just to hang out." He looked away, cheeks turning red, running a hand through his hair. "If you wanna, you could join and bring your friend Henna along."

"Yeah, I'll think about it, but I don't know. I might be busy tomorrow." I said quickly while looking down at the towel in my hand. I didn't want to tell him the truth that my psycho father was the reason I wouldn't be attending, no matter how much I wanted to.

After our conversation in the kitchen, we fell silent

once again. Luckily, it was almost time for customers to be arriving, so I didn't have to bare the awkward silence too long.

I tended to a few customers here and there, and by nine o'clock business was really picking up. I became so busy that I hadn't even noticed Henna had come in until she stood up from her table and beckoned me over. I seated the guests I was with, checked that Jason wasn't looking then scooted over to her table. *What could she possibly want?*

We sat at a table in a corner of the room. Henna sat with her purse at her side and her eyes locked onto my hand as I sat down. I smiled at her and she looked up at me scowling.

"Darn it, Danny!" she said in a harsh whisper and a gesture to my little bandage. She had clearly jumped to the all-to-often conclusion of what occurred last night. "Why don't you call me when something like that happens? You could spend the night with me and my parents, you know. Anytime." Her eyes were distressed as she looked at me. Almost tearing up. I felt horrible. I knew how much she cared and how much she must worry about me. However, spending the night at anyone's house would not fly with my father and I don't want her to get involved for fear that he might hurt her too. I looked into her light brown eyes.

"Yeah, I know. Don't worry about it though. I'm ok. See?" I showed her my hand, all bandaged up. "It's not bad. I fixed it up all by myself." I smiled reassuringly at her. We've been friends for a long time so I'm sure she saw right through it. I changed the subject. "What's up? Is there something you wanna talk about?" She had most definitely seen right through me as she replied.

"Actually, yes. About TNO tomorrow. But I'd rather you told me how you acquired your bandage." I sighed and looked down, hiding my bandaged hand on my lap under the table.

"Henna, I don't really wanna talk about it." I hoped she would just drop it, but I could tell by the look on her face that I wasn't getting out of it that easily. She took my un-damaged hand on the tabletop and looked into my eyes in an understanding way. I knew I could trust her, but I just hated to involve her in it all. I took a deep breath and began. "Well, you know how we were talking about TNO when I stopped for my usual order?"

"Of course," she replied, still gazing powerfully into my eyes. In a hushed voice, I continued to recount the events of the previous night to her, watching as her fa-cial expressions changed from surprise to shock to hor-ror. Her final face was disgust. Disgust with the brute my father was to me and I agreed.

"On a brighter note," this time it was she who changed the subject, "Craig asked me to go to TNO with him." A huge smile peeled across her round face. She flicked her short brown hair as she continued. "I was at work this morning and he just waltzed in, like he owned the place, and came straight up to the counter and asked me." Her voice rose just a little at the end as she said it, unable to contain her excitement. It was kind of cute.

I tried to be happy for her. I tried to look past my jeal-ousy at her fun, happy, normal life, but it was difficult to keep the frown off my face. I feigned happiness for her.

"That's great! He's always seemed like a good guy and I know how long you've had your eyes on him. Congrats."

"Thanks, Danny. I can't wait for the party!" she squealed. Her face started to mirror my inner feelings of sadness. "I just wish that you'd be there too," she said, looking down at the table, defeated.

"I know. You have no idea how badly I'd love to be there. I wish there was a way. I don't know. We'll see. Maybe, by some miracle, my dad'll change his mind or there'll be a lightning strike or—" We both burst out laughing. I realized that I had already taken too much time talking to her, and I gave her a quick hug and rushed back into work.

The rest of that day I was pensive. *Would I really be missing that much if I never went? If I can't even win a battle with my dad about something this simple, would I ever be able to do anything? More importantly, if I did go, what were the consequences when I got home?* As I considered these things, I kept leaning toward going. *Maybe I could sneak out? Or lie? Maybe go with Jason?* He had a car and it would be easy to meet him anywhere covertly and go. My dad would never know the difference. I could tell him I was going to the library, like I do so many times throughout the course of a week. He wouldn't even be suspicious so long as I could get back at whatever time we set. It was perfect, Bill would never know, Henna would be elated, and I could have one night of freedom, one small victory.

I set out on the start of my plan. First, I had to tell Jason that I'd go with him. He'd be pleased, since he's always had a crush on me. I went to the back of the kitchen, where most of the storage is, and found Jason packing and organizing things.

"Hey," I said sweetly. "What'cha doin'?"

"Not much. Why?" He asked, eyebrows raising. My words caught in my throat for a moment. *Was I really about to do this? Just say it, Danica.*

"Well, I decided on that offer you gave me, about going

to TNO with you, and... I think I'd actually like that," I babbled, smiling like a jerk.

"Really?" he said a little too overzealous. It only took him a moment to regain some composure. "Um... cool. So, what time do you want me to pick you up tomorrow?" He asked with a grin. *Crap! I don't know what to say.*

"Er... I guess you can pick me up at six o'clock please... at the library," There was a confused expression on his face, but he agreed.

He shrugged. "Ok. I'll see ya at six then." I smiled back at him and turned to go home for the day.

As I walked towards the bus stop, I started to panic a little. I didn't have much time to make sure my story was concrete. The party was already tomorrow. *How am I going to pull this one off?*

Chapter 3

My story was pretty convincing. My plan revolved around Bill not knowing where I was really going, and I hoped he forgot about the party altogether. I told my dad I was going to the library to check out a new fantasy fiction series I had just heard about and to do some research on careers. He bought it pretty well. Thankfully, because it was Saturday, he was a few alcoholic beverages deep by the evening, so he wasn't exactly lucid. I was packing my purse up, getting ready to go. I stuffed the closest thing I had to a party dress in my bag and a pair of nude colored flats. It was a simple, yellow, knee-length dress that I had gotten for church, although we never went anyway. My dad was too "busy" you could say...busy drinking and smoking and hanging out with a bunch of jerks, just like himself. I also packed up some of my makeup essentials, my phone, my library card in case my dad checked. I took one last look at my drab self in the mirror. Just jeans and a plain Jane t-shirt for now. Lastly, I took a deep, steadying breath, and I walked out into the hall. *It's Ok. He'll never know. I'll be fine.*

I strode into the kitchen, filled with gentle light and an ungentle man. I nodded at him and he nodded back at me, looking up from his newspaper. I opened the door quickly and zipped out into the hall. *Whew, I got passed him. Now I just have to get to the library, get myself ready, and meet Jason. Step one complete.*

I scampered down the hall to the elevator, slipped in and pressed the dingy, ground floor button. On the ride down, I fidgeted and fussed with my shoulder length hair. When the doors opened I practically jumped out. I flew to the doors leading outside and burst through. I felt a freedom I had not felt since I could remember. *I'm outside. Now, I just have to head to the library.*

I headed in the direction of the library. Thankfully, it was not far from my apartment, which did make it easy for my frequent visits. I loved reading. It was my much-needed escape from my daily life. I reached the quaint building and stepped inside. The clerk greeted me politely, as I was basically a regular there, and I smiled, probably more than what looked normal. I went straight to the bathroom to get ready. The clock showed five-forty, so I had a little less than twenty minutes. Squeezing into the bathroom stall, I stripped off my clothes. I got out the yellow dress and jammed my street clothes into my bag. I pulled the dress over my head and slipped on the flat shoes. Stepping out of the stall, I set my bag on the sink counter. Checking the mirror, I was pleasantly surprised to see that I didn't look too bad. The yellow made my hair stick out a bit, but it fit my curves and lean body nicely. Makeup next. Other than covering the occasional bruise, I never got much chance to use my makeup. Bill didn't approve. Tonight, I didn't care. I put on my powder foundation, a little blush, mascara, and a red lipstick Bill never knew I had. I slicked that on last and made a kissy face at the mirror. One last glance as I put my makeup away and I decided I was presentable.

In order to not get a confused look from the clerk, I skirted around behind the checkout counter area and headed out the doors. I started to feel a little nervous, but the good kind at least. Excited jitters. Walking down the library steps, I waited until I saw a guy waving in a car. It was a fancy looking sports car, and in the driver's seat was Jason smiling at me. I smiled back and got in. It was low, so I had to bend in. He kept staring at me as I got situated.

"Hey," he said as I finally was settled.

"Hey. Nice car."

"It's my dad's." He grinned sheepishly. "Let's be real. We know I couldn't afford this off my pizza parlor wages."

"No, I 'spose not." I replied and we both giggled. Then there was an awkward silence as Jason drove off toward the party. I watched out the window for a while at the passing cars and the evening lights coming on in the city. It was calming as my heart was racing. I dared to look over at Jason; he had his eyes fixed on the road. He was wearing khaki pants and a light blue button-down shirt. It went well with his slightly tan skin and brown hair. We had gone pretty far sitting there in silence, but I could see the sign for the ballroom not far ahead and Jason was slowing up. I started a bit when he spoke.

"Are you excited to be going out tonight? Seems like I've only seen you at school or work. That's ok, though, considering I'm pretty much always working too. Barely have time to have any fun," he rambled. I didn't quite know what to say.

"Ha, yeah, I'm excited. And no, I certainly don't go out much... at all really." I replied as we pulled in the lot and parked.

"Well, let's try to make this night count then!" He got out of the car. He was gentlemanly enough to come and open the door for me, which was very unnecessary, but very sweet. Together, we walked toward the doors of the bar's attached ballroom.

Chapter 4

I t was extremely loud inside. I could feel the bass pumping under my feet and rattling through my ribcage. The ballroom was dark. The only lighting was the laser show of the DJ and the dim, warm lights of the bar. The few tables scattered around the outside were lit with candles.

I was struggling to find someone else I knew, when Jason grabbed my arm and towed me over to a group of people, Henna included. They made some room for us and we joined in on the dancing. Henna gave me a playful smile and she showed Craig some of her best moves. Suddenly, Jason grabbed my hand and spun me around. I was already giggling and having a blast and it hadn't even been five minutes. Slowly, I danced my way over to Henna. Talking was difficult with the loud pop music pumping, so she grabbed my arm quickly and led me over to the bar. We ordered a couple of sodas and talked while we waited.

"Aren't you two cute," Henna teased.

"Hey, just 'cause we showed you and Craig up on the dance floor, doesn't mean I like him like that. We're just friends." I retorted.

"Sure," she said with a wink. "Anyways, let's get to the important stuff. Like, for starters, I can't believe you're here!" she squealed. "I don't even care how you did it, I'm just glad that you were able to *finally* have a night of enjoyment." She was beaming as she grabbed our sodas.

"I can't believe it either. It was a challenge and my heart's still racing to even be here, but it was *so* worth it! I'm having such a good time. I never get to do things like this! Thanks for talking me into going." I smiled warmly at her. She was a great friend.

"Of course! Anytime," she replied.

We talked and laughed a little while longer while we drank our sodas. I ordered a light soda with a lot of carbonation and it made my nose tingle. We finished our drinks and turned back toward the dance floor. I couldn't help but smile. It was so nice to be out with friends for once, having *real* fun. Being cooped out in that tiny apartment day in and day out, leaving only when I had a hall pass was a dismal existence. I was just about to hop back out onto the dance floor when Henna grabbed me by the shoulder and spun me back to the counter of the bar.

"Duck down a little!" She said in a hushed voice.

"What!? What's wrong!?" I replied in the same tone.

"I'm pretty sure I just spotted your dad in here! He looked really angry!" Henna peeped.

"Oh no! He must've figured it out!" I squeaked, nearly choking with panic. "What do I do?!"

"Um... I don't know... we gotta get you outta here before he sees you. Let's get you out the bar entrance on the other side of the building."

"Ok!"

With that, we both made a swift and smooth exit toward the bar room and Henna let me go in front of her to block Bill's view. We opened the bar entrance and rushed outside. We had both been holding our breath. We both let it out as we got outside.

Henna was nearly hyperventilating. "Hey, we need to

get you back home ASAP before he finds you."

"I know... What about my stuff in Jason's car?"

"We'll get it later or I can get it to you tomorrow. Don't worry about it now. Here," she said as she grabbed my hand and shoved a wad of cash into it. "Take this and get on the bus. Get home." I didn't argue with her. I took the money and ran to the nearest bus stop. I was lucky that this one was about a block away and around a corner because I had to wait about ten minutes, what seemed like ten hours, to board a bus.

Once I boarded, I went to the middle of the bus and sat, shaking. It was pretty empty with only about four people including myself. I suddenly realized that I hadn't even checked where this bus was going. I looked up front at the screen and it was set to lead out of the city to the last outlying bus stop, somewhere on the edge of suburbia. My mind was reeling. Fear and anger were driving my thoughts. I was so done with living like this.

Chapter 5

I rode the bus for a long while and it was starting to empty as people disembarked. After a while, it was just the bus driver and me. The driver told me that our next stop was the last one before he headed back into town. We continued in silence for about fifteen minutes. The route went out into the suburbs of the city and I looked at all of the cute, cozy houses. Most of them had their lights turned off. The driver finally stopped when we were clear of the suburbs. I asked him if there was any way he could take me farther. He was a kind faced middle aged man. He looked at my desperate face. Checking his watch, he told me he could drive farther out for about ten minutes, but that was all he could do. I thanked him repeatedly and sat back down, in the front this time. During those ten minutes, I could see in the headlights that we were just starting to get out in the countryside with farm fields spotted here and there. He stopped at an intersection.

"This is as far as I can take ya ma'am." He said in an apologetic tone.

"This'll do, thanks so much." I replied. He nodded once and smiled. I smiled back and stepped down. The bus turned to head back to the city. I just stood there, watching the lights of the bus fade. There were no street lights here in the countryside and it was quite dark from clouds blocking the moon. As the bus faded out of sight,

I started to feel a little nervous. During the ride, all I felt was numbness. My mind had gone blank. Now, my mind began to panic and reel as I worked out what my next move would be. I had no phone, which was probably a good thing because then I couldn't be tracked. I had no wallet, no ID, no extra clothes. I laughed as I looked down at myself, barely able to see my yellow dress and flats. *How am I going to walk in this? Oh well.* I still had about ten dollars left from what Henna had given me, tucked safely away in my bra.

My next thought was which direction I should go. I was at a four-way intersection. Straight would lead me the farthest away from the city, so that's what I decided. From what I could make out in the dim light, the road was blacktopped, but well worn. I walked along the graveled road edge and just put one foot in front of the other. I must have walked for about an hour and then, just my luck, it started to rain. I figured I might as well embrace it though because there was nowhere for me to take shelter and I had to keep walking until I found something, somewhere. I allowed the cool drops to fall, hitting my face.

It was at that point I realized the rain was not the only thing falling from my face; warm tears had mixed in too. My pace slowed as I just let the tears and rain hit me. My mind was swimming with panic, dread, hurt, sadness, loss, desperation, and frustration. I didn't know where I was going. I had no plan. *Where would I stay? What if someone saw me?* I also thought about Henna. How I would miss her. She was my rock all these years. The only sunshine in my darkest of days. I thought about her light brown hair, her tender smile, her knowing loving eyes. I was frustrated with myself for taking this risk, for having no plans, for having a tormentor for a father.

Over the course of my life, I have realized that tears of frustration are the hardest to control. Tears of sadness are different, I can control them by thinking of happy times, or at least push them down and tuck them away for later. However, frustration tears are much different. Not only do I feel frustrated, but also sad, helpless, and defeated. I feel as if there is nothing I can do to dig myself out of the mess. I must've been crying for half an hour or better. Eventually, the tears and rain subsided. I just kept on walking. My legs and feet were exhausted, my heels chaffed where the flats rubbed them. I am sure I resembled something like a sad, wet dog. My eyes could just make out that I was coming up to yet another intersection. I had chosen to go straight for each one I had encountered so far, but this one had a gravel road that branched from it. I wanted to go somewhere as obscure as possible, so I chose that one.

I could make out small patches of forest among large open fields. I had no idea what time it was. Probably midnight at least or maybe very early morning hours. I continued to walk the gravel road. I was so exhausted and engrossed in the landscape that I hadn't heard the truck pull up behind me. The headlights reflected off the ground around me and I jumped. Whipping around, I was face to face with an old, dark green, beat up truck. Panic filled me as the truck door creaked open. I was frozen to the spot, like an animal. An older man with shabby clothes and graying hair stepped out and approached me. I was terrified.

"Please... please don't hurt me!" I pleaded putting my hands up to shield myself.

To my surprise, the man chuckled and in a very kind, gruff voice replied, "Hun, I'm not gonna hurt you. Calm down. I was comin' back from a farm supply run in the city and saw you in the headlights. I couldn't believe my eyes to see a young girl out so late at night, all by herself, especially in this weather. You don't look like a late-night jogger, at least not by your outfit anyway." He was slowly approaching me. My heart raced, but something about him seemed kind. "I'm so sorry I startled you but I was concerned. I've a daughter of my own and wouldn't want her way out here by her lonesome." He gave me a gentle smile and I was tearing up again, shaking. "Is your hand ok miss? It seems to be bleeding through your bandage." He gestured to my hand, still up in the air in front of my face. In my exhaustion, I hadn't even noticed it.

In a shaky voice I replied, "Um... yes... I... My hand's ok. I just... I could use some help I suppose." Tears were streaking down my face. "It's just... I have no idea where I am. I've been walking for I dunno how long or how many miles. I just needed to get outta the city." Sobbing now, I continued. "Please, if you could just drop me at the next town or something. Please just don't call the police. I won't cause you any trouble. I..." He stepped closer and embraced me. I immediately stopped crying from the shock of it and just stood there hiccupping and shaking.

"Please don't cry," he said pleading and patting my hair. "I hate it when women cry. It breaks my heart. A woman should never have to cry." He hugged me tighter for a moment. He had a strong, stocky build. Gently, he held me at arm's length. "Listen miss, I won't hurt you, I promise. How about I take you back to our farm and we can get you all cleaned up and dried off. You're soaked to the bone." I was still hiccupping, but I wiped away my tears.

"Okay. I'd like that very much. You're too kind." He led

me around to the passenger side of the old truck. I could see it had only one bench seat and a box with wooden sides. He opened the door for me and guided me in. Then he walked around the other side and got in, started the engine, and we continued down the dirt road. At that point, I just hoped he wasn't a serial killer. He certainly didn't seem like it, but I really didn't have any more options.

Chapter 6

He didn't bother making small talk with me as we kept driving, although he cast the occasional glances my way to check on me. We bumped along dirt roads for hours. I began to see much better in the early morning light. A beautiful mist rolled over the lush landscape. I also looked back over at my driver and I could see he had light blue eyes that looked kind among the wrinkles that surrounded them. He had laugh lines too. His hair was graying. He wore a plaid shirt under some beat up overalls that had dirt and grass stains. I also peaked down at his shoes, a pair of well-worn cowboy boots. As I peered back out through the window, I could just make out a white fence line in the misty morning, then the outline of a barn. We pulled into the driveway of the farmstead. I was in awe. Never before had I seen a place quite so amazing. I took in the beautiful barn, outbuildings, and house, all in tones of gray paint. I could also make out a few horses grazing in the nearest pasture. It was a beautiful place and looked well kept up.

The man came around to my side of the truck and opened the door for me. I hopped out and followed him to the house. The porch light was on. He opened the door and led me inside. Once he flicked on the light, I could see the house wasn't extremely fancy, but it was well taken care of and had a quaint farmhouse style. We entered from the front door into a good-sized living room. The man turned to me and smiled warmly.

"Ya know, I don't think I even introduced myself. My apologies. My name's Maxwell Lancaster. I live with just my son, as my daughter, Amanda, now lives with her husband. And you are my dear?" He had caught me off guard with his question a bit and I had to think for a moment how I would answer.

"Danica, but you can call me Danny," I finally sputtered.

"Danny, it's great to meet you," he stuck out his hand and gave me a firm shake. "Now, why don't we get you some dry clothes? Follow me for a moment and I can take you to Amanda's room. I bet she's about your size. You can pick out whatever you'd like to wear, she won't mind. Heck, she won't even know." He smirked and winked at me.

The stairs were directly ahead of us, gorgeous dark wood, just like the flooring. I followed him upstairs and he led me to the second bedroom on the left. It was not a large bedroom, just enough space with a bed, a nightstand, a pretty white dresser, and a small closet.

"Go ahead and take your pick. It's about two in the morning so you may wanna get some shut eye. She leaves fresh sheets on the bed for when she comes to visit. I'm gonna hit the hay for a little bit yet. Coffee won't be on 'til five. Please feel free to holler if you need me."

"Okay. Thanks so much." I was in shock.

"Of course," he said as he stepped out and closed the door. I just stared at the closed door. It was truly unbelievable that I had landed myself in a nice home, with a kind and generous man... so far at least. I took a moment to close my eyes and thank my lucky stars and take a nice deep breath before turning to look at the closet. I opened the bi-fold wooden doors and found an assortment of cute clothing, as well as a pile of sensible clothing too. The clothes were not mine, so I picked out something that maybe Amanda would miss the least: a pair of worn out sweatpants and a light purple tank top with a horse design on it. Mr. Lancaster was right when he said we were about the same size.

I peeled out of my drenched yellow dress and soggy flats. My feet were so sore and blistered from walking for hours. I rifled around in her dresser and found a plain pair of white socks. I pulled them on, then the sweatpants, then the tank. It felt good to be in warm, dry clothes.

I opened the dark oak door and peeked back out into the hall. Mr. Lancaster was not anywhere to be seen, so I stepped out. Walking down the hall, I saw the door open to a tiny bathroom. Figuring my hair was a disaster and my cut needed tending, I immediately slipped in and shut the door behind me. It had just a simple tub and shower combo, a toilet, and a sink cabinet. There was a white cabinet along the wall for what I imagined was storage, so I checked it out to see if there was a brush or comb of some kind. Just my luck, it appeared that Amanda Lancaster had left some of her belongings behind and I took out a pink hairbrush.

I looked in the round mirror and saw quite the mess. My hair was still damp and matted down. My hazel eyes looked more tired than I had ever seen them. They were red from my crying and my mascara had bled down my cheeks. With my makeup smeared, it was a wonder that Mr. Lancaster picked me up at all. I was really a sight. Getting to work, I used the hand towel to squeeze the moisture out of my hair. Then I combed out the snarls out of my black locks. Satisfied, I wiped off all of my makeup.

Great, now without makeup I look even more tired. I sighed and put the brush back. Then I tended to my bandage. Unwrapping the gauze, I could see that the cut had stopped bleeding. I rifled around some more and found some bandages. I just slapped one of them on and called it good. Straightening out my clothes, I took one last look in the mirror. *Good enough, I suppose.*

I left the bathroom and was back out in the hall once more at the top of the stairs. I went back to my room. I turned on the nightstand light and shut off the main light. Throwing back the cover, I snuggled into the warm bed and turned out the light.

∞∞∞

I woke to the smell of coffee, eggs, and maybe even bacon cooking. That's when it hit me how hungry I had become. My mouth was watering. Cautiously, I crept out of the room and went down the stairs. I had just reached the bottom and looked up. My jaw dropped. The most handsome guy I had ever seen was standing before me, leaning against the wall that divided the kitchen and dining room from the living room. I must have looked like an idiot standing there, mouth agape. He must have been about my age, maybe a little older. He had hazel eyes, dark brown, tousled hair, and a strong jawline. He was probably a little less than six feet tall and broad shouldered. You could see he was muscular even though he was wearing a plaid shirt, rolled up to the elbow. He smiled at me and gestured toward me.

"So, you're the damsel in distress my dad mentioned? You're not what I was expecting, you're much prettier."

He smirked. "My name's Samuel Lancaster." He stepped forward and stuck out his hand. I tentatively reached out and he shook mine vigorously. I couldn't remember the last time anyone called me pretty. I realized I was still holding his hand and my cheeks burned as I let him go. Samuel's cheeks turned red too as he motioned toward the dining table.

Shyly, I sat at the table. It was a bench seat on one side and chairs on the other. Samuel took a spot next to me on the bench. Mr. Lancaster put a plate in front of each of us and put the pan of eggs right on the table, as well as a plate of bacon, bread, butter, and a hefty pot of coffee.

Mr. Lancaster spoke. "Danica, would you like a coffee cup, or can I get you something else? We do have milk as well or—"

"Coffee is absolutely fine, Mr. Lancaster. Thank you. And please, call me Danny." I smiled as he set a coffee cup on the table for me. Samuel was already digging into the amazing spread of food. He passed me the pot of coffee and our hands touched once more. I felt my face get hot yet again. I poured myself a hefty amount of coffee, black. Not usually how I drank it, but there was no cream or sugar on the table and I was certainly not going to impose even more. They had already been so kind. I took a small helping of eggs, some of the bacon and a slice of bread, just enough without going overboard. Father and son began chatting about farm things I didn't really understand. We were nearly done eating when Mr. Lancaster directed the conversation my way.

"Now, Danny, I'm not gonna berate you with questions about where you came from and what you were doing in the middle of nowhere. You seem like someone that needs a helping hand. I'm sure you'll tell us what's going on when you're ready. Further, you may stay with us as long as you need to, but the members of our family have always earned their keep. I don't mean to pressure you, but we could use some extra help in the barn if you'd be so kind. Sam will be glad to show you around," he gestured toward Sam. My cheeks burned again.

"Yes, of course. There's no other way I could repay you for your generosity. Thank you. I just need somewhere to stay for a little while, until I figure out what I'm gonna do." I didn't know how much I should tell them. *What if they told the police? Or worse…*

"And I really don't know much about farming, so I guess Sam'll have his work cut out for him if he's gonna be teaching me," I said, laughing awkwardly. I made eye contact with Sam, for a quick moment. It was the first laugh I had made since last night at the party. It seemed like so long ago now. Sam interrupted my thoughts and drew my attention back to him as he spoke. His warm, deep voice was like honey.

"This farm is our way of life. The chance to share it with you would be wonderful. You'll enjoy the work… I do." He smiled.

"Thanks, Sam."

"As soon as you finish up we're headin' out to the barn," Sam said. We got to work finishing up our breakfasts and I gulped down the rest of my coffee as Sam was getting up from the table. I couldn't help an internal groan as I thought of what I'd just gotten myself into.

Chapter 7

S am led the way into the large, gray barn and I trailed along behind him. I stopped inside the doorway. It was pretty dark in the barn, save for a few windows along the sides. Sam turned on the lights. I was stunned to see two rows of beautiful horses, heads peeking out of stall doors. Never had I been this close to a horse in my life. I always thought how mysterious and majestic they were, and although I was terrified, I couldn't contain my smile.

"They're beautiful." I stated. "I must be honest with you, I've never seen a horse in real life and I'm blown away. How many are in this barn?"

"There are 40 stalls and 33 horses right now. We have a nursery area as well," Sam replied proudly.

"You have baby horses here? May I see them?... Please?" I asked tentatively.

"Yes, you'll get to see them. We have two. However, we have work to do in here first. How about I show you around the barn real quick, where the tools and medicine cabinet are, and I can tell you each horse's name. Then, I'll show you how we muck out stalls." The word "muck" caught my attention. I had an inkling on what that might mean and was not particularly looking forward to it, but if it meant I could earn my keep, I was completely willing to do it.

"Sounds good. Lead the way," I said and gave a curt

grin. I followed him down the concrete alley to the other end of the barn. There was a storage area with totes, barrels, bags, and some pitchforks and shovels. On the opposite side of the storage area was what appeared to be a washroom with a floor drain, a cabinet, and a hand sink.

"Over here we have storage for feed, bedding, tools like this fork—" he handed me a fork with many tines —"and lead ropes, halters, and riding gear along the back wall. On this side—" he turned and gestured to the washroom side, "—is our washroom for the horses, mostly used after a good ride or if they roll around and get muddy outside." He led me over to the hand sink as he spoke. "We also have a sink and this cabinet is the medicine cabinet. Mostly, it's full of horse medicine and remedies, but there's also a first aid kit in here if something were to happen. There's also this small refrigerator that houses medicine that needs to be kept cool, as well as soda, water, or whatever. Good so far?" he asked to make sure I was getting everything.

"Um, I think so," I replied, running a hand through my hair. It was a lot to take in and we were just beginning. Plus, it was pretty hard to concentrate on what he was saying. His jawline, gorgeous hair, and intensely beautiful eyes were quite distracting.

Next, he led me over to the first horse stall. The animal was a striking jet black. Its smooth, glossy coat shone in the sunlight peeking through the nearest window. It had an impressively tall and strong build. It stuck its nose up to me through the open upper half of the door while Sam spoke. I couldn't resist touching the soft, velvety muzzle.

"This is Charlie. He's a Tennessee Walking Horse. Very friendly, as you can see. Charlie's one of our oddball horses. We breed and sell race horses, and he's obviously no thoroughbred, but he's my horse. A local that was selling out of the business sold him to us, it was a pretty good deal. He's a great horse." Sam gave Charlie a loving pat and continued. "If you look above every stall, you'll see there are name plates with their full, registered name, as well as that of their sire and dam. They'll have a long name on the sign above. For instance, this next horse here is named Big Ben, but his full name is Lancaster Bernard Benjamin. Lancaster is our farm name, then his father's name, then his name. His nickname is Big Ben and that's what we call him here in the stable. Don't worry, you'll get the hang of all this." He comforted me, grinning as he must have caught my bewildered expression.

"Yeah, well, I'll certainly try." I said, dragging a hand down my face. He took me through the rest of the barn and named off the horses. We came to the last horse, directly across from Charlie. Sam looked sullen.

"This last one's Clarabelle. She's another oddball here. She's technically a pony, but at the maximum height qualifications of one. She was my mom's horse." Sam turned his gaze away. "She passed away a few years ago from cancer."

I wanted to reach out, to comfort him, but quickly pulled back my hand. "I'm sorry, Sam." That's all I said. He turned back to me and gave me a little smile.

"It's ok. It hasn't been easy. I don't know if anyone really gets over the loss of a loved one. I think we just learn to live with it. But my dad and I are doing ok." He shrugged. "I mean, he doesn't make breakfast like mom used to, but he does alright, wouldn't you say?" Sam grinned.

"He certainly does... And Sam?"

"Yes?"

"I actually lost my mom too... It was a car accident. Drunk driver. My family sure as hell wasn't perfect before it happened, but..." I wasn't sure if I should say more or not. His voice broke my thoughts.

"I'm so sorry for your loss as well. I guess we're two peas in a pod." He smiled a little. "If you ever need to talk about it, I'm all ears."

"Thanks," I replied, looking up at him. *Should I open up?* I knew revealing details would be dangerous, but he looked so trustworthy, so kind. His eyes so warm and welcoming. *Maybe it would be good to tell someone other than Henna and a few details couldn't hurt, could they?* "And...maybe I do wanna talk."

"Ok sure," he said reassuringly. "Why don't we sit for a second, then. How 'bout these hay bales?" He grabbed me around the shoulders and led me to a bale of hay. His embrace was gentle, but still solid and it was truly comforting.

"Well... I remember I really loved my mom. The accident happened when I was just five years old." I reminisced for a second. "My dad, who was a wreck before the accident, just got worse. He already had a volatile personality, and this sent him over the edge." I looked down at my shoes. "He went crazy. He was depressed over my mom's death, and already a heavy drinker...he just went downhill. His aggressions turned to me." My gaze turned to my still bandaged hand. "For years, I've pretty much been my father's prisoner...That's why I ran." A tear went streaking down my cheek.

I jerked back as Sam tentatively reached out and wiped a tear off of my face, but his touch was gentle.

"It's ok," he cooed. "You're safe here. I'm sorry for what happened to you. It must've taken a lot of courage to tell me all of that… At least now I understand why you left. I probably would've done the same thing."

We locked eyes for a moment. "Thank you… You're only the second person I've ever told any of this to. The other is my best friend. She's probably freaking out right now. She thought I was going home…" I trailed off as I thought of her. I also thought of how livid my dad must be. I shuddered. "You see, I was at a party with her last night. I wasn't supposed to go…but I just couldn't help it. I've been under my father's thumb for so long. I barely got to go to Henna's house and to school. Since I graduated, he pretty much let me go to work, the library, and home. So I had Jason pick me up and we met my friend Henna there… I just wanted one night…" I balled a fist in frustration. "But then my dad actually showed up to the party. He must've found out somehow. I don't know how." My throat tightened as I remembered the feelings of last night. "I ran…" I trailed off again. Sam looked a little shocked.

"Wow." His expression changed to that of bewilderment. "That was a lot to take in. I guess I have a lot of questions, but I don't wanna pressure you."

"No, it's ok. I probably already told you more than I should've so what's the damage." I shrugged. I couldn't put my finger on why I trusted this man so much, but something about him just drew me in. I just hoped I wasn't digging my own grave.

"Well, for starters, I gather that you have a boyfriend then? This Jason fellow?" Sam's eyebrows raised.

I eyed him suspiciously. "Er, no. No boyfriends for me. Not with my father. Something about 'boys are the root of all evil or something?' But no, he isn't my boyfriend. He was just kind enough to take me to the party. I actually work with him, or worked rather, since I'm probably gonna be fired for not showing up. Plus, we went to high school together."

Sam looked almost pleased for a moment, but he wiped that expression away quickly. "So if it's not prying, how old are you then? If I did my math right, 18?"

"Yeah. Graduated high school in the spring and have been working away summer saving up for college... then again, I don't even know if Bill was going to let me go to college." I said pointedly. My curiosity turned to Sam. "How old are you?"

"I'm 25. So, yeah, I know I should probably start looking for a grave plot huh?" He winked and I smiled.

"And what about you, I'm assuming you have a gorgeous girlfriend?" I asked.

Sam shook his head. "No. I've had girlfriends in the past, but it never worked out." He ran a hand through his hair as if he was distressed by the topic. "Well, we should probably get to work now, I suppose," he said, changing the subject. "Follow me with your pitchfork and we'll grab a halter and this wheelbarrow," Sam instructed.

I was curious about what Sam was hiding, but couldn't help my thoughts drifting back to Henna. I'm sure she must be worried something happened to me. She thought I was headed home. I felt so guilty about leaving and not telling her, but it was my only chance to escape. *Maybe I can call her?* It would be risky to contact her, but I should at least try. As Sam walked me to the storage area, I decided I'd try to use the house phone later to reach out.

As my thoughts were drifting around, Sam was grabbing supplies; a rope, what I assumed was a halter, and a wheelbarrow. We went to the front of the barn. Sam slid open the stall door and stepped inside. The horse was tall and dark brown. Most of the horses in the barn looked like this one. He slipped the halter over the horse's nose, then ears and fastened it. He clipped the rope under the horse's chin. Sam led the horse out of the stall and I jumped out of the way. Sam giggled at me.

"Follow me. We're taking her out to the paddocks for the day," he said. I scampered to catch up and followed him out of the barn. We continued down a gravel path until Sam stopped with the horse. He gestured to me to open the gate and I obliged, although it took me a moment of fidgeting with the steel chain to get it open. He led the big horse inside, turned her around, took off the rope, and the horse sauntered away as Sam stepped back out of the pen.

"Ok," he said, "now we go back and clean out her stall." We walked back up to the barn and back to her stall. He handed me a fork and grabbed one for himself. "Let me show you how we usually muck out a stall. Melrose's here is usually pretty tidy. She likes to push all of her bedding to the outside of the stall, though." Sam continued to instruct me on the use of the fork and how to clean up the stall. "Once the wheelbarrow's full, we dump it out back on the pile. Think you can handle it so far?"

"I guess so. It's not the work I did back in the city. I bussed tables there, but this doesn't seem too bad yet." I said, but it's not what I was really thinking. I used my fork to sift through the shavings like he showed me, and we made quick work of the stall. The wheelbarrow wasn't very full when we were done.

"One last thing we need to do is to scrape all of the bedding from around the edges of the stall, where Melrose pushes it, back to the middle of the stall. Then it takes some judgement on whether or not we should add more bedding. This may sound stupid, but have you ever cleaned a cat litter box?"

"Yeah, we had a cat when I was little, actually."

"Ok, well, it's kinda like that, only the cat is really, really big," Sam said, chuckling. I laughed too.

"Yeah, I'll say." And we giggled some more as Sam backed the wheelbarrow out of the stall. He stood looking into the stall for a moment.

"Looking at the amount of bedding she still has in her stall, I think we're good and shouldn't have to add more yet. It's something that you just kinda eyeball and you get used to seeing how much a horse needs for bedding."

"Ok. I'll try to pay close attention to what looks good." I said.

"Great! Now only 32 stalls left to go!" he said with a teasing grin. I smiled curtly back, but on the inside I was groaning. However, I knew I had to buck up and earn my keep. Although the task ahead of me would be grueling, at least there was a handsome distraction to keep my mind off the work.

We continued by letting the horses out of the stalls and into the paddocks, and then cleaning out the stalls. We had to dump the wheelbarrow many times. Thankfully, the pile was not that far away. It was a humid summer day and, although there were fans running in the barn, sweat was still dripping off of me.

The last stall was Clarabelle's. She was cute. Her soft coat was mostly a warm honey color with a white stripe on her head, and all of her feet were white. She had a gorgeous, creamy colored mane and tail, and she had tufts of hair coming from behind her shins. I liked her size, too. She wasn't as tall and intimidating as most of the other horses were.

When we were done, we put our tools away and stood for a moment, cooling down in front of a rickety old box fan. Sam grabbed two waters from the small refrigerator and I gratefully took one and gulped it down. It was ice cold and nearly gave me a brain freeze. Sam poured the last few inches of water in his bottle over his face by the sink. I couldn't help but stare as the droplets rolled over his perfectly chiseled cheekbones, down his neck, and into his shirt. He grabbed a towel out of a drawer and wiped his face and neck down quickly, then tossed it into a bin. He grabbed out another small towel and came over by me. My heart stopped as our hands touched a little too long while I took the towel from him. I gave him a grateful smile and began wiping myself off and tossed my towel into the bin as well. I smoothed my hair back into its rightful place too, and he rolled his eyes.

"We just finished mucking out stalls. We're not going to the opera. You don't have to look so breathtakingly gorgeous *all* the time, do you?" He smiled, but he also looked dead serious at the same time. *Did he really just call me breathtakingly gorgeous?*

"Well I'm *so* sorry, but I have to compete with you somehow." My statement was laced with sarcasm. "I mean, are you doing the cover shoot for Hottest Horseman of the Year or something?"

At first, I thought he might have been offended, but then he struck a dorky, dramatic pose like a cover model. We bust out laughing. Sam returned to his normal posture. "Maybe I'd make it into the top five, but not the hottest I'm sure...but thanks, though." He ran an embarrassed hand through his hair.

"Um, you're welcome." I replied awkwardly. I decided to change the subject. "So, are we done for the day?" He looked back up at me, his composure regained. I wrung my sore hands.

"Well, I fed all the horses just before breakfast, so our next task is to—you guessed it—muck out more stalls!" he declared with a big smile.

"Oh, yeah," I huffed.

"Don't sound so excited," Sam jibed. "We'll get to see those foals you were so excited to meet 'cause we'll do the nursery barn next."

I perked up. "That changes things a bit. Lead the way!"

Chapter 8

Sam and I headed toward the nursery barn. It was much smaller than the main one. Once we entered, I saw the foals by their mothers' sides. Small noses and tiny ears accompanied their long, spindly legs. They looked a little awkward, but they were still adorable. I could see there were only four stalls, however, they about doubled the width of the stalls in the main barn, most likely to accommodate the mother and baby. Each stall had an open door in the back to a pasture, so they could go in and out at will.

After letting me gush over the adorable babies for a while, Sam made me get down to business. We entered the farthest stall from the entrance and got to work with our forks and wheelbarrow. Working in silence, we let the rustling of the shavings and the nickering of mothers chatting with their foals pass the time. Occasionally, a foal would come up to me or Sam and nose around on us. Their super soft muzzle tickled my exposed skin. The second foal was already so tall that his muzzle reached my head. He stuck his soft nose onto my neck, into my ear, and then to my hair. Its little chin whiskers tickled so much I giggled like a schoolgirl. Sam laughed and stepped over to gently push the foal away and send him back out to the pasture by his mother. It tossed its head in a silly, awkward protest.

"I didn't want him to start chewing on your hair," Sam

pointed out. "It's not pleasant... trust me." He winked and pulled at a lock of his tousled, brown hair. I giggled. There was just something about Sam that drew me in. Maybe it was just the air of mystery, or maybe it was something more. Either way I couldn't take my eyes off of him. His hair, the way it perfectly accented the shape of his jawline. And his smile, the way it was a little playfully slanted, but so bright and warm at the same time. He must have felt my gaze burning into him because he met my eyes, blushed, and we returned to work. His were the perfect mix of brown, green, and a little blue, all rolled into one. The nursery barn made quick work and in no time, we were done.

"Alright, that was the last stall to muck," Sam sighed.

"Thank God!" I swiped my hand across my brow. We went to dump the last wheelbarrow full of manure. It was exhausting work and I was worn out long ago. My arms were sore and with the heat, I was drenched in sweat again. My stomach rumbled loudly. I looked up at Sam with a little, embarrassed smile. He shook his head.

"Good thing it's lunchtime," he said, dumping the wheelbarrow. "I can hear you've worked up an appetite." He gestured to my rumbly stomach. "Are sandwiches okay?"

"More than okay," I replied eagerly. "I'm ready to eat wallpaper. I can't believe I burned off all that breakfast!" Sam set the wheelbarrow down by the pile and we started toward the house.

"Once you start workin' like a farmer, you start eatin' like one too." Sam patted his abdomen like he was Santa Claus. Truth being that I could tell his abs were rock hard. His sweat drenched shirt stuck to him and showed just the outline of his muscles. I was practically drooling over him once again. I broke from my trance once we reached the porch door and Sam opened it for me. *Such a gentleman.*

When we got in the house, I assisted Sam in preparing the sandwiches. It helped me get acquainted with their kitchen. I buttered bread, grabbed some plates, cut cheese, and I folded the lunchmeat neatly onto the sandwiches, like I had for Bill. We were nearly done preparing them when Maxwell came in. Good thing Sam knew the routine because we had one ready for Maxwell too. He stood in the kitchen archway and smiled for a moment as he watched Sam and I finish up. We put the plates on the table while Maxwell heated up a cup of coffee. Sam and I sat down on the bench again and Maxwell across from us, just like that morning. However the strangeness of it was waning. It felt almost normal to be sitting with them at the table, as if I'd done it many times before. Then again, having a "seemingly" normal family was something I'd longed for a long time.

"What're your thoughts for the afternoon?" Maxwell asked Sam.

"I was thinking I could take Danny and we can work on lead breaking Vera and Lightning some more." I perked up at the sound of my name. "Plus, it'd give Danny a good opportunity to start learning some basics of horsemanship." I didn't get a chance to speak for myself because Maxwell responded.

"Excellent idea! We'll make a farm girl of you, yet." He brightened up as he spoke, almost excited about the prospect. "It's been a while since we've had a farm girl 'round here." He looked off like he was remembering times passed.

"You had Amanda, right?" I questioned. It was Sam

that answered.

"Yes, but not since she got married. She and her husband, Mark, moved away so they could live in the city. He's a doctor."

"Wow," I replied, "That's impressive. I can't imagine all of that schooling. That'd be grueling."

"Right!?" Sam exclaimed. "It's not for me either. I'm perfectly satisfied with my two-year degree."

"What's it in?" I asked

"Equine Science, of course," Sam replied proudly. "It gave me the certification and training I needed to continue the legacy of Lancaster Farm and, hopefully, to improve upon it."

"Sounds like a perfect fit for you, then. I never really gave the prospect of college too much thought... Money was always so tight... But if I could pull it off, I think I'd go for a business or accounting degree. Those are pretty marketable skill sets and I like math."

Maxwell gestured with his coffee cup in hand. "Good point, Danny. Either of those would make an excellent degree."

"And the community college I went to offers those programs. I could help you get set up there sometime... if you wanted," Sam suggested.

"Well, we'll see what the future holds for me, but that does sound great. Thanks." I smiled curtly.

Sam gave me a sympathetic look. It truly astounded me how kind these guys were. Bill hardly listened to me when I spoke, especially of college. He didn't seem to support the idea at all really. He would just brush me off. It was refreshing to have people that seemed to give a damn about me, even though they barely knew me, however, it was a bit unfathomable. I kept waiting for a loophole.

∞∞∞

"Here, you'll need this halter—" Sam slapped a thick nylon rope contraption into my hands. "—and this lead rope." He handed me a rope with a large, metal clip at the end. "I'm gonna have you work with Vera and I'll take Lightning. Vera is a little easier to handle so far," he stated, grabbing his set of tack. "Now, I'm not gonna tell you this is will be easy. It's a challenge, even for me, working with the young ones. I figured, though, that it's a good way for you to jump right in. Like a crash course. Now, you saw me putting halters on the horses earlier, right?" He held up his blue halter.

"Yes."

"Great! So, small opening for the nose, larger side goes up behind the ears, then this strap goes under the chin and clips behind their cheek up by the ear." He demonstrated. My mind was desperately trying to keep up. "Then, clip the lead rope on the bottom." He pointed out the metal ring on the bottom of the halter. "Ready to give it a shot?"

I smiled like a loon. "Not really, but do I have a choice?"

Sam just chuckled. He patted me on the back as we strode out of the barn.

Time to go make a fool of myself, I thought as we walked through the barn doors and started on the gravel path toward the paddocks.

We reached the pasture for Vera and Lightning. Sam nimbly opened the gate. As it creaked open, he pointed out Vera for me. For young horses, they were already so very tall. Vera had a dark brown coat, black mane and tail, and her legs darkened to black. Lightning was slightly lighter brown, also with a black mane and tail, brown to black legs, and a skinny, white streak down his nose. They were beautiful, outlined against the soft blue sky and short, green grass in their pasture. The two young horses saw us approaching and they promptly moved away. Sam called out to them, but to no avail.

"They're a little 'spirited.'" He raised his eyebrows. "Sometimes they'll come to you, other times you have to wear them out first. Do you want me to show you?"

"Yes, please," I replied. I had no idea what I was doing so I was eager to let him go first.

"Alright, so I'm probably gonna have to try a few times. Lightning can be stubborn. What I'm gonna do is approach him and try to slip the halter over his face. The trick is to get him to stand still long enough for me to do it. And you have to approach them in a way that makes them feel comfortable, rather than like they're being hunted. It takes some finesse." He winked at me and strode off toward Lightning.

It was mesmerizing, watching him work. He knew all the right moves to get the horse to surrender to his will. He was smooth and calm as he walked toward lightning with his body angled slightly away from the young horse. Lightning would pull away a little, but each time Sam got a bit closer. It was like a graceful dance. Eventually, Sam worked his way close enough and they both stood next to each other for a moment. Sam moved slowly as he went to slip the halter over Lightning's nose. Lightning reacted a little bit but allowed Sam to slide on the halter and clip it together. Sam snapped on the lead rope. Then, he and Lightning headed back toward me. The young horse tossed his head a little and pulled back some, but Sam didn't flinch. He just kept the same calm grip on the lead and kept walking towards me with a face of determination. They made it back to me faster than I'd hoped. It was my turn.

"Okay, go for it," Sam said with a smirk on his face. Lightning was wiggling around at Sam's side.

I felt like I was being thrown in the deep end. "Uh... wish me luck."

I started tentatively toward Vera. I was terrified. Vera was tall, even at a distance. Horses were beautiful, yet quite intimidating. As I walked, I knew I needed to get over my fear and put on the same air of confidence that Sam did. That looked like it was a large key to getting this right. Plus, I had to attempt not to startle her.

I approached her on the side and got about ten feet away before she sauntered slowly away from me. We played cat and mouse for what seemed like a lifetime. I was beginning to get frustrated and worn out. I gave Sam a pleading look.

"Try walking backwards toward her," he shouted.

I stared at him in confusion but shrugged my shoulders and gave it a shot. Turning my back toward her, I approached carefully, trying not to trip on a rock. I looked over my shoulder and was shocked to see that it was working. When I was just a few feet away from her, I turned around little by little. Her eyes got wide, but she didn't run off. I spoke softly to her.

"It's okay, sweetheart. I won't hurt you." I had the halter open and was able to slip it over her nose, then I got the part over her ears, and then secured the clip on the side. It was clumsy, but she put up with it. Finally, I clipped on the lead rope. I gave a little squeal of success and Vera jumped.

"Oh, sorry, Vera," I said in a calmer tone. "I didn't mean to spook you." We walked back toward Sam. She pulled against me a bit, but I kept the same confidence and determination Sam had and tried not to let her shenanigans faze me. We reached them, and Sam looked impressed.

"Wow, you're a natural!" he proclaimed. "I don't know what you were so worried about." He patted me playfully on the shoulder.

"Ha, very funny. That was hard!" I said, exasperated. Sam laughed at me. "Why did walking backwards even work?"

"Sometimes, animals don't really understand that we're walking towards them when we're facing away. It just plays a trick on their mind," Sam replied as he closed the fence.

"Neat. Where to next," I asked. Sam took the lead with Lightning.

"We're going to the outdoor arena to practice pretty much what we're doing now. Maybe try putting a saddle on Vera. We'll see. I'll teach you how to lunge them, too, so we can burn out some of their energy a bit. They behave better when they're worn out. We're basically gonna try and work on making them mind, rather than pulling back on us and tossing their heads or rearing up, which is the game they're playing now," Sam said as Lightning pulled back, almost on cue.

"Okay. Hopefully, Vera stays as good as she's being for me." I looked back at Vera calmly walking alongside me.

"Hopefully," Sam said. "I've been working with her a little more than Lightning. She started her training first."

The arena was a sand lot in a rectangular shape, with

a white wooden fence lining it. It had a red gate at both ends. Sam opened one up and let me go through with Vera. She tripped on me a bit as she walked in. Her and I were both a little awkward getting our coordination working together. Sam strode in with Lightning and casually shoved his lead rope in my hands.

"Here, hold him while I grab a lunge line and lunge whip." I grabbed the rope and suddenly I was stranded there with not one, but two huge horses while Sam went to get supplies. My nerves prickled as I stood there with the two animals all by myself. I did my best to tamp down the panic. Thankfully, Sam returned quickly.

"You take Vera on the far half of the arena. Just walk her in a large circle. If you want her to stop, you can say 'halt' or 'whoa' and if you want her to walk again say 'walk.' If you wanna try backing her up, pull back toward her chest a little on the lead rope, put a hand on her chest and say 'back.' She should know those commands by now. If you want, you can set up the poles that are in the corner—" he gestured toward the white poles with black rubber bottoms in the far corner "—and space them apart enough to have her follow you through in a zigzag pattern. Just mix it up a little so she doesn't get too bored with it. I'm gonna take Lightning on this side and lunge him. Then, we'll switch, and you can watch me for a bit while I lunge Vera. Just so you can see what that's about. Good deal?"

"Yup, I think I can do it. No guarantees, though. If I mess up your horse, it's not my fault." I held my hand up innocently. Sam smiled and shook his head.

I sucked in a big breathe to help me over my inner panic and got to work. Luckily, Vera worked well with me and she seemed to enjoy the challenge of going through the poles I set up. She was very eager to please. It was amazing to see this huge animal respond to my commands. It was empowering, not something I typically felt. I peeked over at Sam a few times and watched the ease and grace with which he worked. He was running Lightning in a large circle, giving him commands as he went. Sam stood at the center and had a certain angle of his body toward Lightning that drove the horse onward.

We switched horses and I stood with Lightning and watched Sam start off Vera on the lunge line. He had the same angle to his body as before and used the long whip to just touch her rear while he gave her a command to walk.

"You see," Sam said, "the trick here is to position your body behind their front shoulder to drive them forward." I looked at the special angle he held toward her front shoulder. "The rope and cues from my arm keep her moving in a circle around me. I have to keep turning or moving around so I'm always at this angle. Then, I can give her commands like walk, trot, and canter." I must've looked a little confused because he explained further. "Walk, trot, and canter are 'horse speeds' essentially, and in that order. There's also a gallop which is usually the fastest gait. Usually a four-beat step, but you probably don't need to worry about that anytime soon."

"They say you learn something new every day. If that's the case, I'm gonna need a book to start writing all of what I learned today. Because it's A LOT," I confessed. Truthfully, it was all a bit overwhelming, but watching Sam with the horses made me believe it might all be worth it.

I continued to watch him lunge Vera for a bit then went to work with Lightning. He was a bit tough to handle. Lightning spent a good amount of the time controlling me instead, pulling away from me, stopping, trying to walk in front of me or on top of me, and tossing his head around. I'm sure we put on a great show for Sam's entertainment.

When we were done working with the two horses, it was late afternoon. We led Vera and Lightning to the main barn where Sam brushed them off. Sam took each to their stalls and then put away their tack. He had me keep my lead rope.

"We get to go collect all the horses we turned out this morning. Then, it's feeding time," Sam pointed out. Luckily, most of the horses knew exactly what time of day it was because they were gathered at their gates, eagerly awaiting us. Sam swiftly took two large horses at a time. I, of course, took just one, and my palms were still sweaty. We had to go back and forth a few times to collect them all. Then it was feeding time.

"We're lucky on this farm," Sam began. "We have automatic waterers. All you'll need to do is go in each stall and check 'em, cleaning if need be, while I do the grain. In the winter, we feed them hay daily, but while they're on pasture, we don't have to worry about that as much." Sam went to the back of the barn and grabbed a rolling cart with bins on it. They seemed to be filled with different kinds of grains and scoops. I looked into each one. Some of them had a sweet, earthy aroma, which was new and strange to me, but smelled heavenly all the same. Kind of like the smell of the horses, you just can't get enough, yet you don't know why.

He grinned at my fascination with the grain but carried on with his duties. Sam rolled the cart up to the first stall and unlatched a special feeder built into the pen that swung out on a hinge. It could be filled and then turned back into the pen again. The horse was preoccupied with what Sam was doing so it was easy for me to open the stall door to check the water. We continued along down the line. I had to reach into a few of the waterers and grab out wet, slimy hay or grain particles. I gagged a bit. It was a gross, but I didn't want Sam to think less of me.

Once we finished feeding, Sam handed me a large broom and he and I swept the alley. We swept the dirt right out the door. I handed my broom back to Sam, and for a moment, our fingers touched. Our eyes met in embarrassment. Sam flushed and quickly averted his gaze as he went to return the brooms.

As he walked off, I listened to the horses happily munching on their grain while Sam put our brooms away. It was a very calming white noise. I took in a big breath of the scents of the barn, which were kind of musky, but also sweet and somehow calming. *Someone should make a candle out of this.* Sam did a once over of all the horses before turning out the lights. He motioned me out and shut the barn doors behind us. The sun was on its way down on the horizon as we headed for the house. Not quite sunset, but close. All I knew was that we were on the verge of dinnertime and the sleep my body craved so much.

Chapter 9

As soon as I walked through the door of the house, I flopped down onto the couch like I owned the place. I was exhausted. Sam had worked me hard throughout the day. He walked into the kitchen and was pounding down a tall glass of water when Maxwell came in. He was sweaty and tired looking too.

"Well, kids, what are we doin' for dinner?"

"Pizza," Sam huffed out as he flopped down on the couch beside me. "It's easy and I'm tired."

"Hm, that does sound like an appealing idea." Maxwell pondered with his thumb and forefinger around his chin. "I'm wiped, too, and cooking does sound like a process right now."

"Then, I second that decision," I put in. I was too exhausted to think about cooking or helping anyone else cook.

"How about we do pizza, and then popcorn while we watch a movie?" asked Sam.

"Oh, my God, Yes!" I exclaimed. "That sounds great!"

"Okay, deal," said Maxwell. "I'll preheat the oven and get two out. Sam, wanna make the popcorn?"

"Sure, no problem." Sam huffed. He dragged himself up off the couch. He got out the popcorn maker and two large bowls. Maxwell unwrapped the pizzas, so they were ready to go and then sat down in a leather recliner alongside the couch. I felt a little useless at that point, but I was too tired to care. Maxwell turned on the TV and handed me the remote.

"Here, pick something out. Anything you like." He had brought up their satellite TV guide. There were many channels to choose from, but I was somewhat familiar with them since we had cable back in the city. I smiled and nodded at Maxwell while he got up to put the pizzas in. I chose a movie channel that was playing a comedy. I was in the mood to laugh a little after an insane night and day. Maxwell took out the pizzas, and the heavenly aromas of cheese and sausage drifted under my nose. I scurried over to the dining table and took my seat next to Sam at the dining table. We dug in hungrily. Working hard throughout the afternoon, I hadn't realized I was quite so ravenous. It was still oven hot and nearly burned my mouth, but I didn't care. It was so good; the best comfort food. Sam poured me a glass of milk and I guzzled that down too. We ate quickly and quietly, all of us tired and starved from the day's labors. When we were done, we picked up our plates and put them in the sink.

Sam started doing the dishes, so I grabbed a towel to dry and he gave me a warm, grateful smile. Maxwell went to sit in his recliner with a magazine in hand. I had to frequently ask Sam where things went, but I got the hang of it after about halfway through the dishes. There weren't many to do with just the three of us. We finished up and then Sam poured a little butter over our popcorn with a dash of salt, mixed them up, and brought one big bowl to Maxwell and I puzzled as, rather than one of my own, Sam had one big bowl for him and I to share. We sat together on the couch again. Nothing but the bowl in between us. The popcorn was delicious. I had never had homemade popcorn before. Just the stuff from the bags. This brought it to a whole new level. Come to think of it, we didn't keep real butter in our apartment either, just the margarine. I reached in for another big handful to shove into my mouth, but accidently brushed hands with Sam. Our eyes shot up to meet. Sam smirked and pulled his hand away, gesturing for me to take my heaping handful. Blushing, I took my popcorn and then diverted my eyes back to the movie.

I barely knew him, yet something about him just drew me in. And was it just me or was there something between us? Every time we locked eyes the tension that hung between us was almost palpable. *How he could possibly be interested in a common scrub like myself?* It was beyond my comprehension. I was just so average, so blah, and he was just so... not. Even the guys back in high school, who I considered fairly handsome, never paid me any attention. And they couldn't even hold a candle to Sam's glamour. He was the total package, the way he held himself, his slightly deep, warm voice, his perfectly tousled hair, chiseled jawline, the vibrancy of his hazel eyes. He was a ruggedly irresistible cowboy.

I tried to keep my attention to the movie. I reached for some more popcorn when Sam and I brushed hands again. My cheeks flushed, and he gave me a playful sideways smirk. This time we lingered there a little longer. But again, he let me take some popcorn first. His gentlemanly gestures were brand new to me. He seemed a little old school that way. Always ladies first, holding every door, every gate for me. I was a little off put to be treated so well. It was definitely not something I had ever been used to, but I certainly was not complaining.

We were about halfway through the movie when, to

my disbelief, Sam pulled the oldest date trick in the book. We had just finished our popcorn, and he set the bowl aside. Then, he did a big yawn, arms raised and all, kind of obnoxiously, and set down his arm "accidentally" right around me on the top of the couch. He even scooted the tiniest bit closer to me. If that wasn't a blatant sign of his interest in me, I didn't know what was. My cheeks burned red and my eyes got wide. I was in shock. I sat there rigidly for a moment trying to get my bearings. Was I supposed to lean in? *I don't even know this man.* However, something about it did feel right. The whole evening had felt right, like I was meant to be there, like I had been there forever. It was so perfect and felt so normal. Yet, I couldn't help but wonder if this was all too good to be true. No matter how kind they seemed, these men could still be dangerous. I needed to be careful and tread lightly until I knew more.

By the end of the movie, I didn't even know what it was about. I hadn't been paying attention at all. My mind and body were way too preoccupied. However, Sam broke away from me when the movie was over, and I saw Maxwell getting up too.

"Well, it's nearly bedtime," Maxwell stated. "Danny, if you wanna take a shower, you're more than welcome, of course. Not the best water pressure, so we can wait for you first. You deserve it after all you went through last night and the heat today. There should be towels up there in Amanda's bathroom. Just holler if you need anything, OK?"

"That sounds great." I stood up and turned towards the stairs, then turned back. "Thank you guys again for being so welcoming." My cheeks flushed once more. I was so embarrassed to be living in their home, eating their food, using Amanda's things. I felt like a freeloader, even though I had put in a good day's work.

"Don't worry about it. We loved having you here today," replied Sam with the slightest tinge of red on his cheeks.

I smiled back and went up the stairs to the little bathroom. I cranked on the faucet to the shower and was grateful for the warm steam that began to fill the small room. Next, I peeled off my dirty, sweaty clothes and left them in a pile on the cool tile floor. I checked myself in the mirror. It wasn't an awful sight, but not great. My hair was a little messy, my face slightly dusty from the arena sand. Suddenly, I heard laughter coming from downstairs. I cracked open the door slightly, so I could hear better. It was Sam that had chuckled. He was talking to Maxwell.

"Dad, seriously, I just can't wrap my head around it." He giggled a little more. "I've never met a girl quite like her." I could hear Sam pacing around on the wood floor. "What's scary is that I haven't even known her for twenty-four hours and already she leaves me speechless and breathless." he said, exasperated. "And don't give me that look, I know she could be trouble, Dad. I'm not that naïve. You know, maybe this is her MO. She grabs men by the heart and works her way in and then just when you're least expecting it bam!"

Maxwell chortled. I could hear him patting Sam. "I know son, I've got a good feeling about her and I want to believe she's telling us the truth, but we do have to be careful. We don't know anything about this girl."

"I know. And I know I said I'd never fall in love again. Not after Brittney. But, I don't know... maybe."

"Well, I tell you what. I know I'm going to get a call to

do hay in the next week here and I'll do some investigating in the city and see what I can dig up." I shuddered at Maxwell's idea, but I knew there was nothing for him to find other than what I told him.

"Sounds like a good idea. I'll let you know if I notice any red flags while I'm working with her. We gotta try and give her the benefit of the doubt though. If she's telling the truth, she's been through a lot," Sam pointed out. "And this stays between you and me." Sam whispered.

"I agree. We'll see what I turn up with. Hopefully nothing, but we can't be too careful," said Maxwell.

I stopped listening in and carefully closed the door. Stepping into the shower, my mind was reeling, and my heart was racing. What I had heard had shocked me in several ways.

I stood under the water and tried to figure things out. *Sam really was interested in me. They're suspicious of me too, but does that put me in danger? I'd been honest with them so there should be nothing to worry about... right? And what if these guys are the real deal? I'm already starting to fall in love with the place. Can I take that chance?*

It would be risky, but I needed to get word to Henna. She'd know how to get me out of this mess. But how was I going to do it right under the Lancaster's noses?

Chapter 10

I rolled over in bed and looked at the clock. It was still early in the morning, long before Maxwell or Sam would be up. Throwing back the covers, I crept out of bed. The moon was enough to see by as I searched the top of the nightstand for a pen. Nothing. I gently pulled the nightstand's drawer open. Just as I had suspected, there were some lose notes, a journal, and a pen. I took the pen and journal. Upon opening it, I found that it had barely been used. Just some leftover chicken scratch notes from Amanda's childhood. I turned to the back to find a clean, empty page.

Dear Henna,

Hey, it's Danny. I know you're probably freaking out right now, but I'm okay... I think. You've also obviously figured out that I ran away. I don't think you'd blame me. You know better than anyone what I've been through. Let me fill you in.

I rode the bus out of the city and walked for miles. Then, this older guy, Maxwell Lancaster, picked me up. He seemed nice and, honestly, he was my only option at the time. He took me back to his horse farm and he and his son, Sam, have treated me well so far. In fact, I'm kind of into Sam. But, one can never be too sure. I know they're suspicious of me. I heard them talking.

I'm hoping you'd have some ideas on what I should do. I at least wanted someone to know where I am. I'll leave the address at the bottom of this letter. I would've called, but I am afraid the police may be tracking your phone if Bill reported me missing. Plus, I don't want to freak out the Lancasters. I hope this finds you well and that I can see you soon.

All my love,

Danny

I quickly scribbled the address at the bottom and folded up the letter. Now, to find an envelope and stamp. I remembered there was a secretary's desk near the bottom of the stairs. But, that meant sneaking out past Maxwell's room and they were already suspicious. My palms grew sweaty as I headed for the bedroom door.

I held my breath as I eased the door open. It made no noise. Tenderly, I crept out into the hallway. My pulse was racing. I felt like everyone in the neighborhood would be able to hear my heart beating wildly. A few more steps to Maxwell's room. Using just the tips of my toes, I inched my way passed. I stopped at the top of the stairs to listen. Silence. No one was stirring. I gingerly put my weight on the step. It made a tiny creak and I froze. Holding my breath, I listened. Still nothing from Maxwell's or Sam's bedrooms. Taking another deep breath, I gathered all the bravery I could muster and tiptoed my way down the steps, every creak sounding like a thunderclap.

I made it to the bottom. No rustling of the men. *Whew!* I scurried to the desk. It was full of old newspapers and junk mail. I sifted around until I found some small drawers. I tested one. It didn't make much noise, so I began rifling through them until I got lucky.

Using the stamps and the envelope I found, I hastily scribbled out Henna's address on it. Slapping the stamp on, I crept my way to the front door. I knew this one would be the biggest challenge of all.

The front screen door usually made quite the racket. I sent up a silent prayer and slipped on my shoes. My sweaty fingers grasped the cool, silver handle. Turning the knob, I pushed lightly on the door, bracing it with my other hand. It creaked just a bit. I bit my lip. No one stirred, but I knew I couldn't make much more noise, so I abandoned my shoe to hold the door open as I scampered down the steps to the grass. I ran to the mailbox as fast as I could and stuck the letter in. I put up the flag so the mail carrier would see it, praying neither Sam nor Maxwell would notice it.

Sprinting back I stuck my foot back in my shoe and drew the door shut inch by painful inch. I put my shoes back and regained control of my breath. Once I stopped panting, I began my ascent of the stairs. I crept passed Maxwell's room. Slipping like the breeze back through my bedroom door, I scrambled to the bed and under the covers.

My ears strained to listen. One minute. Two minutes. Then, I heard someone stir. My pulse hammered. It was Sam. *Oh, no! He must've heard the door!*

I squeezed my eyes shut and waited for him to burst into my room. Nothing happened. My ears followed his footsteps. He strode passed my room and headed down the stairs. *What if he thinks I'm still outside? What if he sees the mailbox?* I sucked in a breath and strained every fiber of my being to hear him. Then, I heard the clink of a glass, the rush of water from the kitchen sink. *Maybe he's just getting a glass of water.* I kept listening. Soon, Sam came up the stairs and went back to his own room. I finally let my breath out and prayed Henna would get that letter.

Chapter 11

I handed the halter to Sam to return to the hook. His hand lingered on mine as he took the tack from me. I gave him a smirk. In the week that I had been at Lancaster Farm, I had found no evidence that Sam or Maxwell were cold blooded killers. Of course, it takes longer than a week to get to know someone, but I knew already that Sam's interest in me was, maybe dangerous, but not lethal. And despite all of my fears, I had to admit to myself that I liked his subtle attentions.

Henna would approve too. He looks like one of the jocks she'd reel in. Thinking of Henna, I wondered if she'd gotten my letter. I'd watched as the mail car had picked it up. Neither of the Lancasters had ever noticed the flag.

Sam pulled me out of my thoughts as he returned carrying a saddle. "Hold out your arms," he instructed.

I obliged and took the heavy saddle. He started adding to the pile. Sam grinned at my exasperated face as he tossed on a bridle and blanket.

"Are you going riding?" I inquired, following him as he walked away.

"No. You are." His smile was wide as he threw back Clarabelle's stall door.

I could feel my eyes widen. "But Sam," I pleaded, "Surely, I have more groundwork to learn. I mean, what if I fall off and get crushed? Plus, they go so fast—"

"You're not gonna fall off and get crushed. I won't

make you go fast." Sam rolled his eyes at me. "As a horse-man, you either conquer your fears or they conquer you. And if you're going to stay here, which I hope you do," he glanced into my eyes, "you'll need to learn to ride. And Clarabelle isn't that big. She's just a pony," he patted her lovingly on the neck.

"But, Sam, she was your mother's horse... I couldn't."

"Yes, you can." He said sternly, but then spoke in a softer tone. "I want you to. She'd be a perfect match for you... You have a lot in common with the woman my mother was. Clarabelle deserves to be loved and to get back in the arena and back on the trails. I can't think of anyone better suited to take on my mother's horse. So please, will you do this for me?" His eyes grew big and round like a puppy. I couldn't say no to them. I broke.

"Okay, I'll try. But, only for you." I gave him a stubborn smirk.

"Thank you," he said, beaming with pride.

Sam held her steady while I threw the saddle over her back. It was a good thing Sam had already been made me practice saddling for him on the taller horses because saddling her was pretty easy. I left the cinch hanging by her belly while my clumsy fingers slipped the bridle over her face and her soft, delicate ears. She stood as still as a statue for me. Next, I tightened the cinch on her belly. Then, I had Sam check to make sure everything was in order, especially the tightness of the cinch, which is hard for a beginner like me to gauge. He pulled it a little tighter.

"Okay, you're good to go," he said. "Now, you're gonna mount on the left side, so grab the reins at her withers with your left hand, and then, with the same hand, grab the saddle horn," he demonstrated. "Then, left foot in the stirrup, take a big hop up, and swing your right leg over Clarabelle's rear. Be careful not to bump her with your foot," he warned. "Then we can adjust your stirrups again."

Shaking with nerves, I grabbed the reins and saddle horn, then put my left leg in the stirrup and hoisted myself up as I swung my leg over her rump. I was shocked that I had made it as I settled into the saddle seat.

"There you go! See? You're just fine." Sam patted my leg. "Your stirrups are set a little too long, so I'll adjust them for you quick." He unbelted the stirrups and raised them up a bit on each side. "There, now you're good to go. Also, make sure to keep good posture and hold the reins between your thumb and forefinger with your wrists up."

"Okay," I replied, adjusting my grip.

"We're just gonna start off with a basic walk. And don't worry, I'll be right here the whole time." He smiled up at me.

"Sounds good." My voice shook.

"Go ahead and tell her to walk, and if you need to, give her a little nudge with your heels. Make sure to keep your toes pointed slightly up with your heels downward." I gave him a confused look. "I know it's a lot, but you'll get the hang of it. Clara is very forgiving. Now, give it a try."

"Okay," I sighed. "Walk," I instructed Clarabelle and she proceeded at a slow, steady pace. Sam followed close by us. Her walk was very smooth.

"See?" Sam mocked. "You're doing great."

I just shook my head. We had made it all the way around the arena.

"Now take her for a figure eight pattern. Use the reins and gently roll your hand, on the side you wish to turn, in toward you. That'll pull the rein in. At the same time, lay

the opposite rein against her neck. She knows how to follow these cues."

I nodded and pulled in the left side rein while putting
the right side against her neck. She responded by slowly
turning left. Then, I repeated the process only on the
right side this time, then finished off the pattern with another left turn.

"Great," said Sam proudly. "Now, say 'whoa' as you
gently pull back both reins to get her to stop." I did as he
commanded, and she slowed to a stop.

"Well, how are you doing so far? Wanna go faster?"
Sam inquired.

"It's going much better than I thought. I guesss this
isn't *so* bad." I was grinning from ear to ear as my nerves
began to calm.

"Well, then, let's have you make her trot. That's the
second gait. It'll be the bouncy one you may have seen
me do a little."

"Okay, let's do it," I replied with building excitement.

"Tell her to walk again. Then, tell her to trot and give
her a little nudge with your heels." I told Clarabelle to
'walk' and waited until I got past the curve. Then, I gave
her a nudge with just my heels and told her to 'trot'.
She responded and began a slightly faster, bouncy step. I
nearly bounced out of the saddle.

"The next step is to try what's called 'posting'," Sam
called out to me. "Basically, the trot is a two-beat gait
that you can make easier on you and the horse by rising
up a few inches off the saddle with one beat and then sitting back down the next. A rule of thumb to use is to 'rise
and fall with the leg on the wall.' So, when Clarabelle's
outside leg moves forward, you rise up off of the saddle.
Then sit back down on the next beat." I made an attempt

at it and it did make the trot a little more bearable. I went up and down with the beat of the horse. Her gait kind of pushed me up out of the saddle anyway so it wasn't too hard to understand.

"You're getting the hang of it!" Sam called from across the arena. I was pretty proud of myself, too, at making such good progress. I went several laps around the arena, practicing my posting skills. Clarabelle and I trotted up toward Sam and I slowed her to a walk, then halted next to him. He looked up at me. "Nice job, Danny."

"Thanks." I replied bashfully. "Can you hold her while I hop off?"

"Sure." He grabbed the reins and held her steady while I lifted my right leg over her rump and stepped to the ground. My thighs were tired from the posting. It felt like I had just done a hundred squats which, basically, I had. Sam handed me the reins and walked over to open the gate for me. I led Clarabelle through.

"Take her down towards the wash stall. We can tie her up and you can take off her tack and brush her down good, and get some practice picking her feet," he said, as I walked her toward the barn. "You've seen me do it, so you should be able to handle it, right?" he asked, as he caught up with us.

"Ah, I guess so," I responded.

I brought her up to the two ties in the wash stall and we switched her into a regular halter, slipping off her bridle underneath. Then, I clipped on a rope on each side of her halter. Next, I undid the cinch and slid the heavy, hot leather saddle off and into my arms. I walked across the alley and returned it to the rack. Sam handed me a soft-bristled brush and we each took a side and brushed the sweat and dirt out of her soft, honey colored coat.

The action was very calming and methodical and her scent was musky yet sweet. Once we were done brushing, Sam tossed me a hoof pick.

"Start on her front feet," Sam instructed, "and work your way around from there, just like you've seen me do. Bend down by her front leg and grab onto her... er, ankle... and say 'up' so she knows what you want her to do." I bent down by her front left leg and grabbed her a few inches above her hoof and told her 'up.' She immediately lifted her foot and I used my back to help her support her weight a bit.

"Okay, now what?" I asked.

"Now take your pick, and scrape out any debris in a downward, gentle motion. Here, like this," he said as he bent down beside me, put his arm around my back to support himself, and took my hand to guide the pick. My hand tingled where he touched it. Sam's head was right next to mine as he was speaking. I don't think he realized how close we were. My pulse thundered in my veins. I found it increasingly difficult to pay attention to what he was saying.

"Go from the back of the hoof to the front. Be gentle so you don't injure the inner portion here called the frog," he said, pointing to the fleshy part of her hoof.

"Got it, thanks." I said breathily. I looked up and found myself nose to nose with him. Our eyes met, my heart stopped. Tension hung in the air like a fog. I glanced down at his soft, pink lips. In that moment, I thought he might kiss me, but he just bashfully smirked and stepped away. Embarrassed, I snapped my concentration back to picking Clarabelle's hooves. Sam observed at a distance, but I could still feel the tension.

When I was done, I put the tools away and then unclipped Clarabelle from the ties. Sam opened up her stall door and we put her back in before gathering the rest of the horses. We made quick work of feeding the horses and checking water. I stepped out of the barn and Sam turned off the lights and shut the door behind us.

The sun was sinking behind the barn, framing the big building in a beautiful orange horizon. A perfect backdrop for a perfect day. I stood there for a moment, mesmerized by the beauty, then turned and followed Sam up toward the house.

Chapter 12

I had just come out of the shower after dinner and Sam was standing in the hall awkwardly. Sam looked at me and seemed to go into a trance. I realized I was wearing only a towel around my body. Finally, he regained his bearings.

"Ah, well," he stammered. "You've been here for a couple weeks now and we've done basically nothing, but work like dogs, so I was wondering if you'd want to accompany me to a bonfire tonight?" he sputtered out. He was desperately trying not to look at me. His cheeks were bright red.

"Of course!" I said, giddy. "Sounds like a blast! I've never been to a bonfire before."

"Great!" Sam exclaimed, his cheeks still pink. "I'd suggest just wear a sweatshirt and jeans is all. And I found a nice pair of tennis shoes in my sister's closet. Hopefully they'll fit you."

"Thanks, Sam. What brought this on all of a sudden?" I asked suspiciously.

"One of my good buddies from high school texted me today and pretty much asked if I was dead." Sam smirked. "Needless to say, I've been neglecting my friends recently. I've been a little... preoccupied," he looked up at me. I flushed. "But, they asked me today if I'd come out to their fire tonight. So, I thought I'd run it past you."

"Well, it sounds like fun. Um, I'm gonna get dressed

now." I had been awkwardly standing there in the towel.

"Oh, of course!" Sam spluttered. "I'll just meet you downstairs."

I grinned as he walked away. Scurrying to my room, I quickly got dressed. My nerves pricked with excitement. I'd never been to a fire before. *Henna would be so jealous. I wonder what's taking her so long to reply.*

I dashed my worries away as I popped out of my room and bounded down the stairs. Sam was wearing a handsome red flannel, jeans, and a nice pair of tennis shoes. He grinned at me. Maxwell was in the kitchen preparing his dinner. He gave us an intrigued look, one eyebrow raised.

"We're headin' out to a bonfire for a little while tonight. Out behind the Johnson's farm," Sam answered his father's inquisitive gaze. I was waiting by the door.

"Alright. You two have a fun time, but be safe please."

"Yeah, will do, Dad, thanks. See you later," Sam replied as we walked out the door.

We headed to the older garage on the farm. Sam strode over and threw up the garage door, revealing a stunning car inside. I hadn't seen Sam's car before. He had always taken the farm truck to go get supplies and groceries and he rarely had time to go out. I stood off to the side as he backed the car out. It was an old 50's car with a slick, black paint job and black leather interior too. I'm not going to lie, it was sexy.

Once he had backed it out, I hopped into the passenger seat. Sam beamed. My cheeks burned under his intense gaze. He must've realized he was staring and averted his attention to the radio. He tuned it to a county station. Sam was tapping along with the beat on the steering wheel as we headed toward the driveway. It was at that moment I realized I had not left the farm property since I had arrived, which seemed so long ago. I looked out the window thoughtfully as we passed farm fields of corn and hay. The sun was nearly set, save for a red line along the horizon, now behind us. The moon was out too, although not yet bright. We hadn't gone more than several miles away from the farm when we turned down a gravel road. The little pebbles flung against the underside of the car and clinked against the metal. We came upon a large, white farmhouse and a big red barn. Sam turned in the driveway. There were other vehicles parked behind the barn. We drove around the back and parked next to them. From the car, I could see little calves next to tiny calf houses by the barn. Sam came around and opened up my door. Stepping out of the vehicle, I heard the gentle lowing of cattle.

We had parked next to the edge of a hay field. There was a trail through the middle of it and some woodland at the back of the field. My eyes could just glimpse the fire blazing just inside the tree line.

"C'mon," said Sam. "Follow me." I was a bit surprised as Sam took my hand and led me toward the trail. His hand was warm against the cool summer night. There wasn't a cloud in the sky as the stars were coming out. Sam's cologne wafted under my nose as we walked side by side. I inhaled deeply. We approached the tree line and I could see a small group of people gathered around the fire. That's when I got a little nervous. I realized I wouldn't know anyone.

Everyone greeted Sam as we entered their circle. They all seemed happy to see him, like he was the life of their party.

"Everyone, this is Danny," Sam began. "She's a family friend from the city."

"Sure, she is," a young man jibed.

"Danny, this jerk is Jeff," Sam retorted. Jeff stepped forward and firmly shook my hand.

"Nice to meet you. Allow me to introduce you to the rest of the crowd. This is my girlfriend, Stacy, my older brother, Jeremy, my sister, Jada, and her boyfriend, Tucker." I felt Sam's had tense in mine at the mention of Tucker. I looked up at him, but his face was composed. "Finally, we have our friends Dylan and Ava Davis." Jeff finished.

"Nice to meet you all. I'm terrible with names so my bad if I mess them up," I said, apologetically.

Sam and I took a seat on a log. I was glad introductions were over, they are always so awkward. The fire was warm, cozy, and burning bright. Sam grinned at me and took my hand again. He gave it a gentle squeeze. My heart fluttered.

He continued catching up with his friends, never letting go of my hand, however. I tried to act casually like he was, but I kept glancing down at our interlocked fingers. *Was this some kind of sign? Is he sending me a message?* I attempted to draw my attention back to the conversation. I had never seen Sam with his friends before and I wanted to see how they interacted.

"How's the dairy going?" Sam asked.

"You know, the milk price could be better, but we've still got food on the table, so can't complain," Jeff responded.

"Got our second crop of hay off last week," Jeremy interjected. "Just glad we got it up before the rain. You know how that goes." He grinned at Sam.

"Right! Tell me about it. Our horses can't have anything that's been rained on. We aren't taking any chances on mold," Sam replied.

"Have any good sales lately?" Jeff inquired.

"Some," Sam answered. "My dad's been running most of the sales. You know how particular he can be. But, we've had some high rollers interested in our stock and even some interested in stud prospects so that's promising. It's always nice to get some cash flow."

"Awesome. Can't complain about that," said Jeff. "I almost forgot, can I get either of you something to drink? Sam, a beer?"

"You know me too well," Sam replied. Jeff tossed Sam a can and he caught it with ease. Then, Jeff turned to me. I had no clue what to ask for. I'd never really had alcohol.

"Um," I said stupidly. "Oh, I don't know." I think Stacy saw my helpless, nervous look, and she responded for me.

"Grab her a wine cooler, Jeff. Those are always good." She gave me a wink and a sympathetic glance.

"Yeah, sounds good. Thanks," I said, mostly to the girl. Jeff went into a cooler and then walked around the fire to give me my beverage. I'm glad he didn't throw it. That would've failed epically. My hands were sweaty from my nerves and I was struggling to open the bottle. Sam noticed my fumbling, and I gave him a pleading look of defeat and handed him the bottle. His hands were big and arms so muscular, he twisted the top off with ease and smiled smugly as he handed it back to me. I stuck my tongue out at him playfully as I took the bottle back. I was surprised at the taste when I took a sip. It was sweet with a little nip from the alcohol, but not much. It was dangerously good.

Sam started cracking jokes and telling stories. Everyone was so focused on him. Like he really was the life of their party. It was heartwarming, but I was a little jealous. I had never had friends like these. I'd only ever had Henna. I loved her dearly, but to have a group of friends like this would have been amazing. Everyone gets along. Everyone knows each other's ins and outs, how to make each other laugh. Dylan spoke up and broke into my thoughts.

"I love this song. Hey, Jeff, turn the tunes up."

Jeff cranked the knob of the radio. Ava got up and found an open spot to dance in the firelight. Jada followed. Stacy was about to go over to them but turned and came my way. I wanted to go hide under a rock.

"C'mon, Danny! Dance with us," Stacy invited. She grabbed me by the hand. I grumbled but figured it would be a good idea to make friends. Getting up the courage to break away from Sam's side, I went to join them.

I'm glad I did because it was a blast. The girls were so welcoming. Not at all like the ones had I gone to school with who were cruel and catty. I noticed that, although the boys had gathered closer together to talk, their eyes were more concentrated on us. You could tell they couldn't help but stare. I caught Sam's eyes several times and we both looked away bashfully. However, when I'd glance over at Sam, I also noticed Jada's boyfriend Tucker staring at me. Blatantly staring. It was a bit unnerving, but I tried to just shake it off and have fun.

When the slow songs came on, we'd sit down to quench our thirst. I just sat with the girls and listened to them talk about their daily lives and town gossip. It was so much fun to hear what a different world they grew up in compared to me. We were up dancing again and then another slow song came on, but this time a few of the guys came over and began dancing with their girlfriends. I stood alone awkwardly until someone grabbed my hand and swung me around.

I gasped, but quickly realized I was in Sam's strong arms. I followed his lead and we just slow danced by the fire. My heart thrummed away in my chest. The alcohol was making me a little bit more awkward on my feet. I looked up at him and he smiled down at me warmly. I laid my head gently against his chest. His heart was pounding hard, too. He switched it up and put his arms tightly around the small of my back and pulled me in a little closer. I reached my arms up and around his neck and let them rest against his muscular shoulders.

My eyes widened as I saw Tucker heading straight over toward us. More like stumbling over to us as he seemed quite inebriated.

"Mind if I cut in Sam?" His question sounded more like a jibe.

Sam's whole body tensed. "I do mind, Tucker," he replied sternly.

"Awe, c'mon. We're just here to have a little fun!" Tucker clumsily reached for my hand and began to pull me away from Sam. I struggled out of his grasp and Sam positioned himself between us.

"That's enough, Tucker." By this time our altercation had finally caught the other's attention and I could see Jada making her way over.

"Why do you gotta be like that, man?" Tucker slurred over his words. He gave Sam a shove and Sam stumbled back a step.

"Tucker, stop," Sam demanded.

Tucker shoved Sam again. "What's the matter, Sammy? Afraid I'll steal this one from you too?"

Sam flinched at those words as if they stung him. But he didn't bother to reply. He just reached behind himself and protectively pulled me in closer. At the same time Jada was trying to drag Tucker away.

"Okay, Tuck, I think we've overstayed our welcome. Let's go home." If she was upset with him, she didn't show it. Jeff came over to help her and they each took an arm. He stumbled along toward the path with them.

Sam turned around to look me over. "Are you okay?"

"I'm fine. But, what was all that about?"

"Let's sit down and I'll fill you in."

Everyone settled back down. The fire flickered before us. Sam put an arm around me and pulled me closer.

He began his explanation. "So about Tucker. He, well, I guess I should start at the beginning." Sam seemed like he was struggling to find the words. "I was with this girl, Brittany, for a couple of years. I thought everything was perfect and that I was in love. But, love can be blind and I found that you can't always trust your heart… You see, I wanted to ask her to marry me before my mother passed as she was getting sicker and I wanted her to be around when I got married. But… the night I was going to ask for her hand, I found her in bed with Tucker." Sam was staring into the fire.

"They obviously aren't together, but that's something I could never forgive," Sam continued. "And I haven't been with anyone since. I don't know if true love is really out there for me, but I also don't know if I want it. Not when love comes with so much pain."

I didn't quite know what to say. Maybe there was no right thing to say.

"That's awful, Sam. Cheating on someone… it's just not right. But, I do believe there is true love out there for all of us." He looked back up at me and I stared deeply into his eyes. They looked pained, but he smiled and pulled me in for a brief hug.

"For your sake, I hope you're right," he began. "You deserve someone to truly love you with everything they've got to give."

"Thanks." I smiled at him and gave his big hand a gentle squeeze. His eyes started to soften and I could see the corners of his mouth turning up too as he looked at me.

The fire was beginning to die as it was getting late into the night. Slowly, couples were heading out and going home.

Pretty soon it was just Jeff, Stacy, Jeremy, Sam, and me. We sat quietly together, watching the remnants of the fire. I'm sure we were all feeling the buzz from the alcohol, I certainly still was. I snuggled in closer to Sam as the cool night air crept in. Resting my head on his chest, I listened to his heartbeat and the low rumble of his voice as he spoke across the fire to Jeff. Slowly, the flames turned to embers and put me in a trance as I watched them dance around the coals. The talking seemed to die off again with the last of the embers and Sam turned my face up to his.

"Should we call it a night?" he asked, his eyes glittering in the moonlight.

"Sounds good." I sat up. Sam stood and gave me a hand to stand.

"We're gonna head out then, guys."

"Okay. It was good to see you, man. It's been too long," Jeff replied as he got up and patted Sam on the back.

"That's for sure. Hopefully, we can do it again soon."

"And it was nice to meet you, Danny." Jeff tipped his ball cap to me.

"Yes, nice to meet you, Danny!" Stacy chimed in.

"Thanks guys, pleasure to meet you, too."

We started to make our way down the trail. Sam's fingers found their way into mine. He held my hand the whole way. Sam opened the car door for me and I slipped in. He got in and started the engine. We began on the path toward home.

"Did you at least have fun tonight?" Sam ventured.

"Yeah, it was different, but fun. The girls were really welcoming. Jeff's girlfriend saved my butt when she suggested the wine coolers. I kind of choked when Jeff asked me what I wanted. I haven't really had alcohol before. And sorry I didn't talk much, I couldn't speak farmer like the rest of you," I teased.

Sam snorted. "Don't worry, you'll get the hang of farmer talk. I'm glad you had fun, though." He squeezed my hand reassuringly.

I could see our farm as we pulled up. The yard light shone on the barn and made it easily recognizable. We pulled into the drive and I felt the immediate relief of being home. Sam pulled the car into the garage and we just sat in the car for a moment. Sam turned to me and I looked over at him. His gaze burned right through me. He looked like he wanted to say something, like he was holding something back. I gave him a puzzled look. My mind clicked on what he was thinking about as leaned slowly in toward me. My heart nearly beat out of my chest.

He glanced down at the seat and then back up into my eyes mere inches from his. I looked down at his lips. His hand gently found its way to the back of my neck and drew me in. Our lips only brushed at first and then they met with fire. His kiss sent chills down my spine. I kissed him back and ran my hands into his hair. He wrapped an arm around my waist and pulled me closer.

He placed little kisses along my neck that sent lightning bolts through my body. I moaned and he pushed his body up against mine as we slid lower in the front bench seat. Our breathing got heavy. I shivered as his hands found the bottom of my shirt and just as they started to pull it up I jumped back. He abruptly pulled back.

"I'm sorry," he breathed. "I didn't mean to push you. I know you've been through a lot in life. This is probably the last thing you need..." He looked at my lips and then looked away shamefully. I was still panting.

I ran a hand awkwardly through my hair. "It's not your fault. And I'm not saying I didn't like it. It's just a bit too much too fast. I mean, we barely know each other... And I don't exactly have a good history with a man's hands on me, but... maybe we could take things a little slower?" I looked at him hopefully. "I... I do really like you, Sam."

His dazzling eyes met mine and his shameful scowl turned into a grin. "I've got to be honest with you. I really like you, Danny. Something about you struck me the moment I saw you. Maybe it's fate, but... I can't make any promises. It's been a long time since I've been in a relationship and I don't know if that's what I'm looking for. I promise I'll be gentle with you if you'll be gentle with me?" His eyebrows were raised and he wore a sideways smile.

"Deal." With that I pecked him on the cheek.

Chapter 13

T he next morning, I woke up and went down for breakfast to find Sam and Maxwell already at the table. My head hurt a little bit. I reached for the coffee and sat down by Sam. Deciding to skip the sugar, I just drank it black. I took a big gulp and looked over at Sam. He was watching me already and he gave me a playful smirk. A little relief flooded through me. Clearly, I had not imagined what had happened last night. I raised my coffee cup to him in response. Maxwell spoke and broke our trance.

"You guys ok?" he said as he sat down.

"Yeah," Sam hastily replied.

"Yup." My eyes darted away, and my cheeks flushed.

"Ok." Maxwell sounded suspicious of us, but he didn't say anything more, he just gave us a little eyebrow raised glance. Sam split the, now awkward, silence.

"So, I was thinking of doing a little trail riding today and putting some training time in for Vera and Lightning."

Maxwell looked concerned. "Sam, she hasn't been riding that long. Give her a chance to get her bearings before you take her out of the arena."

"Relax. We'll go on the sand trails just past the barn, barely into the corner of the woods, not far. She can handle it." He looked over at me proudly.

"Just be careful," Maxwell replied. Sam was still looking at me.

"I will," he responded.

"By the way," Maxwell continued, "I got a call last evening that there is hay ready for pickup. Sam, I know you know the scoop, but Danny—" my attention snapped up to him, "—that means that I'll be leaving this morning and I won't return until tomorrow mid-morning with the load." He turned his attention back to the two of us. "You two will be in charge of the farm while I'm gone. Think you can hold down the fort?"

Sam waved him off. "Of course. This time, I won't be alone. I'll have my partner in crime here to back me up." Sam gave me an affectionate glance. My thoughts drifted to the fact that I'd be truly all alone with Sam for the first time.

"I'm sure we'll be fine," I chimed in. "I've learned a lot and I'm capable of doing some of the farm tasks on my own now. We should be okay. As long as there's no crisis." Raising my brows, I took another big gulp of coffee.

∞∞∞

"All good," Sam said as he finished checking Clarabelle's cinch. "Here, I'll give you a hand up." I stepped into the stirrup and he helped hold me steady as I swung my leg over her rump and settled into the saddle. She stood forgivingly still for me.

"Thanks," I said as he patted my leg and headed for his big horse, Charlie.

Sam easily stepped up and gracefully swung himself into the saddle in one fluid movement. I could see Charlie was excited to be out and about for the first time in a while. He was pulling at his reins a bit and stomping his feet around eagerly.

"Now, we're not going far, just past the paddocks, onto some sand trails, and up into the corner of the woods a bit. Then, we'll take a break and head back. Clarabelle is an old veteran of these trails, so she should do most of the work for you. And we're just gonna walk, mostly."

"Sounds good, Captain," I said with a playful salute. Sam rolled his eyes and we started off on the gravel path through the paddocks. The gentle rocking of Clarabelle's hips was relaxing, and I started to let her do most of the work. She fell right into step on Charlie's right side, slightly behind his shoulder. I let my mind wander as I listened to the horses' footfalls on the gravel, and then in the sand. My eyes drifted along the beautiful scenery: the tree line in the distance in front of us, the swaying, green grass in the pastures, all against a cloudless, cerulean blue sky. *I could look at this view forever.*

Then, my eyes drifted toward another version of beauty. They wound their way up and down Sam's figure. He had on a short-sleeved button up shirt and a stylish brown cowboy hat. My mind drifted off to the steamy scene from the night before. Butterflies fluttered through my body at the thought and I bit my lip.

The sand path became rougher as we neared an incline that lead to the woods. I was wondering how the horses would scale the slightly rocky rise, but Charlie made it look easy and Clarabelle handled it with grace as she stepped up the hill. I was the one who was a bit off balance going up and had to adjust so I didn't fall backwards out of the saddle. We broke through the trees at the top of the rise. The ground leveled out as we made our way on a narrower path. Tall trees only let in patches of sunlight, scattered on the forest floor. The air smelled moist and earthy in the forest and was significantly cooler. It was refreshing. Birds and squirrels were chattering all around us.

The path wound through the woods. I could hear water gurgling somewhere up ahead. My suspicions were confirmed when entered a clearing with a small creek running through it. Sam pulled up to the creek with Charlie and hopped off. I did the same with Clara, and Sam helped me out of the saddle. My body tingled where his hands touched me. We left the horses to relax and sip the water, as they were a little sweaty from the summer heat.

All around us were green leaves and moss-covered trees, the soothing sound of the creek flowing over stones, and gentle, filtered sunlight glittering on the water. It was a serene spot. I just stood there and took it all in. This is something I would never had gotten the chance to see in the city. Maybe that's why I had always loved the park by the apartment so much. It brought me a little piece of happiness.

"Pretty, isn't it?" Sam's voice broke into my train of thought. He had been observing me.

"Yeah, it's a lovely spot." My cheeks flushed a bit and I began to twiddle my fingers.

"Not as lovely as you, of course, but it's one of my favorites here on the farm. There's a spot further up into the hills that I'll take you to when you're more ready for a long trail ride. You'll really enjoy that one." He was stepping towards me a bit and my heart started to race.

"Can't wait. I'll need to practice quite a bit more on Clarabelle. I nearly fell off up the hill." I giggled awkwardly and stepped to lean up against the tree next to me. He gradually closed the distance between us and put a hand on the tree close to my shoulder. Sam was right in front of me — so close I could feel his breath. My heart started to thunder and anticipation ran through my veins.

"Don't worry about it. I fell off loads of times when I was learning to ride. You're starting off way better than I did, and I had been learning from my parents since I was born. Before you know it, you'll be an old pro. But, I've actually discovered something else you're pretty good at." Sam gave me a mischievous look.

"Oh, yeah?" I said suspiciously. "What's that?" He leaned in so that our lips were nearly brushing.

"You're a pretty good kisser." I didn't get a chance to respond as Sam gently pressed his lips against mine. He wrapped his other hand around the small of my back and drew me in. My heart stopped. Passion stirred within me and I kissed him back hard. Our chemistry pulsed like lightning from his veins into mine. My hair stood on end. He pressed gentle, sweet kisses on my neck that sent chills down my spine. I threw my hands up into his hair. We devoured each other.

Sam slowed the passionate kisses to soft, light ones, pressed sweetly to my lips. They may have been gentle, but they were still intense. They gave me more goosebumps. Sam pulled away, slowly, to look me in the eyes. We were both breathing a little heavy. He looked me up and down and bit his lower lip.

"I know we're trying not to rush things and I don't know if I'm looking for anything serious." He ran a hand through his hair. "But, gosh, it's so hard not to."

"Oh, stop it." I pushed him away playfully and stepped toward the horses. Sam trailed behind me.

"What?" he inquired. "You're gorgeous, Danny. You're

the kinda beautiful that doesn't need to hide behind a mask of make-up." He stepped in front of me and turned my chin up to look him in his serious eyes. I pulled away again and giggled awkwardly. I really didn't know how to take a compliment. No man had ever said such things to me.

"Yeah, well, you're this Mr. Perfect, handsome stud that's way out of my league," I huffed.

"Well... I wouldn't say Mr. Perfect, but..." He gave an obnoxious, teasing smile, while he posed like Hercules. I rolled my eyes so hard I could almost see my brain. I continued on my little rant.

"And besides, you barely know anything about me. I could really be a raving lunatic. Or what if I was a total brat, just really good at hiding it?" My hands were waving in the air frantically. Sam grabbed my wild hands and steadied them at my sides.

"Then give me the chance to get to know you." His voice was serious and pleading. I ran a hand through my hair.

"I just... I've never really had a serious boyfriend before." I felt so embarrassed.

"Oh, so I'm your boyfriend now?" Sam's eyebrows raised.

"Shut up." I teased and shoved him playfully away once more.

"Hey, I'm not asking you to be anything you're not. I just want the real Danny. From the little bits I've seen of her, she's smart, funny, kind, and hardworking...for a city girl, that is." He grinned and pulled me into his chest.

"Hey! I worked in the city!" I looked up at him, protesting.

"Oh, really? Do tell."

"I worked at a pizza parlor. Waitressing, you know, bussing tables and taking orders, and such. Wasn't great, but it was something." I leaned into him as I began to reminisce on my old life.

"Wow, they must really whip waitresses into shape because you're great here on the farm. I mean, those heavy hay bales are kicking your butt, but you're *pretty* good," he chuckled. I looked up at him and stuck my tongue out. I returned my head to his chest and listened to his heartbeat. We stood there hugging and he started to sway us from side to side.

"Sam?"

"Yeah?"

"Do you *really* think I'm pretty?"

"Danny, I meant it when I said it. But I'll tell you as many times as you need to hear it. You're beautiful."

A tear fell from my watering eyes. He was so wonderful. *How did I get so amazingly lucky?* I knew it was too soon, but I swear I loved him. It almost rolled off my tongue, but I bit it back. He picked my chin up.

"Hey, don't cry." Sam's face scrunched in concern.

"I'm okay," I said, pulling away and wiping my tears. "I'm just a little overwhelmed."

He looked guilty. "I'm sorry, I didn't mean—"

"It's not you... It's me. I just... this just feels too good to be true." I started sobbing. "You don't understand." I crumpled down to sit on the nearest log. "I'm not used to being treated this way. You're so kind, gentle, and caring. It's so alien to me. I mean...it's awesome, don't get me wrong. But, my mind and body just don't know what to do with it. I just don't know how to process this." Sam joined me on the log. "With Bill, I lived every day in fear. And I wasn't allowed to have a boyfriend of any kind. If

I strayed from the path he set for me, it was met with severe repercussions. I'm not used to the freedom. I'm sorry... I'm sorry that I'm damaged goods..."

Sam wrapped me in a hug. "Hey, no, you're not damaged goods. You've become the biggest light in my life since my mom passed. And I'm not perfect either, not since Brittany threw my heart away and stomped on it..." He paused, pondering. "You're like an angel who's woken me from a deep, dark slumber. I promise you, it'll be okay. I'll do my best to make you feel safe and protect you... I... I love... I..." he stuttered and trailed off. Instead, he just grabbed my hand and gave it a gentle squeeze.

After a while, he stood up and went over to the horses. I just sat there frozen for a moment. *Did he just nearly say 'I love you'?* My mind was blown. It occurred to me that maybe we were both damaged goods, kindred spirits.

I numbly stood and walked over to Clarabelle and gave her soft muzzle a kiss. Then I threw my arms around her for a hug. There was something about the horses, so calming and healing. Sam checked the cinches. I broke away from Clara and walked around to get into the saddle. Sam helped me up. Then, we started the short trek home in silence.

∞∞∞

When we finished putting Clarabelle and Charlie away, it was time for morning chores since we'd left on our ride right after breakfast. Sam decided we could make better time if he did the main barn and I did the maternity barn. I didn't mind. It would be nice to have a moment to myself.

I headed to the maternity barn and went into the small feed stall. I stood in the doorway for a second and just breathed in the scents of horses and sweet grains. My thoughts became a whirlwind. *He almost said, 'I love you'! I mean, it's not that we don't know each other fairly well now. I trust Sam now. And I think I do have feelings for him.* My heart was aflutter. I didn't know what exactly was holding me back. It was probably the years of conditioning to be afraid of boys and to stick to the straight and narrow that Bill instilled in me. Kind of hard to get over that with just the snap of my fingers.

I grabbed the grain bucket and scoop. My fingers lifted the metal latch for the feeder and swung it out to fill it. I did the same for each of the feeders and returned the bucket and scoop to the feed stall. Then I walked to the back of the stall and grabbed the scissors off the hook on the wall, leaned down, and slit the twine on the bale of hay.

The glint of light off of the scissors brought the last memory of Bill's abuse flashing through my mind. The stinging pain, the sight of my blood, and the knife. I dropped the scissors and stumbled backward until I was up against the opposite wall, hyperventilating. *He doesn't control you anymore, Danny! Pull yourself together! You deserve to be happy! Let the past remain in the past.*

I regained control of my breath and steadied my shaking hands. I straightened up and smoothed out my shirt. Gritting my teeth with a new resolve, I bent down and picked up the scissors. I took a breath and finished cutting off the bale's other string, then returned the scissors to their hook. Grabbing the flakes of hay, I finished feeding the horses.

My arms had gotten stronger since being at the farm and I threw the hay into the stalls with strength. One of my favorite foals came up to the stall door and I kissed his soft muzzle. His breath was warm as he nuzzled me. I looked into his eyes. They were dark brown with many black and golden flecks in them. He nickered at me and I smiled. I gave him a final pat and strode over to shut off the lights. As I shut the door, I met Sam leaning against the door frame. He was waiting for me. The door clanked shut behind me. I broke our silence.

"Hey, I'm sorry about earlier. I didn't mean to freak out on you." I tucked a strand of hair behind my ear as I looked down at the ground.

"It's okay. You can freak anytime you need to. I'm here for you." He smiled as he shrugged it off. "Shall we get started with Vera and Lightning?"

I was tightening the cinch on Vera's saddle. Not aggressively tight, as we wouldn't be riding them. This was one of their first few times of having a saddle on. The idea was to just get them used to it. Sam swung the saddle up onto Lightning's back and Lightning scooted forward, a bit startled by it. Sam held him firmly by the lead and spoke softly to him. Once Lightning's dancing feet calmed back down, Sam reached under his belly for the cinch and tightened it. He had me hold Lightning as he checked the tightness of my cinch.

"Nice job. That's perfect, Danny."

I blushed. "Thanks. I'm getting better!"

"Pretty soon I could start calling you a cowgirl." Sam

winked.

I took Vera a good distance away from Sam and we both began to lunge our horses. I was beginning to get the hang of the angle behind their shoulder and was able to keep Vera going at a steady pace. She was doing really well, too, and didn't even seem to be bothered by the weight of the saddle. Her graceful hooves were gliding over the ground and her thick mane was flowing out with the breeze. I could hear Sam give Lightning a little bit more direction. Lightning had a stubborn streak and always needed an extra push. Sam was helping him get on the correct lead. Vera was still doing well. I pushed her a little harder and asked her to canter. She obliged and started her easy, three-beat gait.

I loved listening to the hoof beats. It was like music. *Thrump, thrump, thrump.* I asked her to slow to a trot and watched as she bounced around me. Then a walk. Finally, I asked her to come to a halt.

"Whoa," I called firmly to her. She respected me and came to stand. I walked up to her and rubbed my hands all over her, telling her how good she did. Sam was having some difficulty making Lightning canter. Vera and I stood side by side and watched the boys struggle. Sam had to keep putting the pressure on Lightning, getting close behind his front shoulder. He cracked the end of the whip on the ground behind him. Lightning gave a little buck out with his back legs. I giggled at his spunk. Sam scolded him a bit and Lightning finally broke into a canter. Sam kept pushing him harder until Lightning was racing circles around Sam like a tornado, kicking up dust in his wake. By the time Sam started to slow him down, they were both winded.

∞∞∞

"Gosh, he was being such a butt head." Sam complained as we began to lead the two horses down the gravel path.

"Just takes after his mentor." I stuck my tongue out at Sam, who returned the gesture.

"All I have to say is that he better turn out to be a good racer. Usually, the ones with the most attitude end up being pretty good." He opened the gate for us.

"I think he'll be fast. He was whipping around you in the arena today." I slipped the halter off of Vera.

"True," Sam replied, sending off Lightning. "He definitely needed to burn off some of that spunk." Sam shook his head at the young horse. Lightning snorted as if he heard us. "They're like children." Sam ran a hand through is hair.

"Yeah, actually, they do remind of two little kindergarteners testing their boundaries."

"Oh yeah, big time." Sam huffed. We leaned against the gate. "Say, do you want kids someday, Danny?" His question caught me off guard. I contemplated for a moment.

"I suppose so. I hadn't really thought too much about it. That would mean getting married and I hadn't really put that into the picture yet either. But, I think so, yes." Sam nodded. "What about you?"

He turned to face me. "I do, but, so far, it just hasn't been in the cards for me. Marriage and the whole works, you know?" Sam came a little closer, "Although, I'm beginning to come 'round to the idea again." Sam blushed a little and looked at his shoes.

I knew I should've maybe been stunned by that statement, but I wasn't. I turned to him and squared my shoulders. "You know, that's the funny thing. Standing here with you, I actually *could* picture that kind of future and dream a little. Raising little rug-rats on this beautiful farm... What a glorious life they would have...

"Even if it's just a wild fantasy, it's still a big leap from what I used to dream about. The only things I ever considered before were finishing high school, getting a job, and helping Bill pay the rent." I shrugged nonchalantly. "Nothing beyond that. I had no vision of a future for myself... Didn't believe one was even possible. No life goals." I stared out at the cerulean sky. "I just assumed I would live a boring, dreary life, with a sad, old man, and someday fade away into nothingness." My gaze turned back to Sam's bewildered expression and I smiled big. "Now I'm actually happy to think of the future and its endless possibilities. There is so much I could accomplish... Maybe more if you were by my side." My fingers traced his hand.

Sam scooped me up and set me on the fence. He kissed me with such passion, I felt the tingle all the way to my toes. My heart raced faster. He sent kisses wildly down my neck toward my chest. His hands were strongly holding me steady. My arms wrapped around his neck and I squeezed him in closer. Our lips locked again and again, each time sending more chills through my body. Then, just as suddenly as we had begun, the kisses slowed down to pecks and then Sam pressed his lips against my forehead. He pulled me into his chest in an embrace. I listened to the beat of his heart, thrumming fast.

We were silent for a few moments while we reined in our heavy breathing. Sam set me back on the ground.

"You know what?" Sam prodded.

"What?" I placed my hands on my hips.

"We have to get our behinds going on evening chores before the sun starts setting." He tossed me my set of tack. It hit me in the chest and I caught it in my forearms.

"I know. What's been taking you so long?" I mocked as we started toward the barn.

"Well, if someone's lips didn't keep mysteriously falling onto mine, we wouldn't have this problem." He gestured at me as if I was the culprit.

"Good point. When I find whoever's doing that, I'm really gonna have a firm talking to them. They shouldn't be putting their lips on my man." Sam's eyes rolled so hard I could almost hear it.

We were nearly to the barn doors when a flashy, silver sports car pulled in the driveway. I recognized it immediately.

"Henna!" I shouted as I dropped the tack and bolted for her car.

Chapter 14

Tears were steaking down my face as Henna stepped out of the car. I threw my arms around her and I felt her sobs too.

"Danny! Oh, my God! Are you okay?" Henna held me at arm's distance.

"Yes," I said between sobs. "I'm fine. I'm good... It's so good to see you."

"It's good to see you too. I'm so glad you're safe. I was so worried about you. You sounded a bit scared in your letter." I shot a glance at Sam. His eye brows raised, but he remained silent. "I thought they would've done you in by now. I'm so sorry it took me so long to get here, but I had to make up a good story so my dad wouldn't be suspicious and I had to arrange for Jason to tag along just in case... I mean... I didn't know what to expect, so I thought maybe backup would be necessary." Henna glanced at Sam and I peered over her shoulder at Jason. I hadn't even noticed he'd gotten out of the car.

I snapped out of it. "My apologies. This is Sam. Sam, these are my friends Henna and Jason."

Sam stepped forward to shake their hands. "Yes, welcome. She's said good things about you both." There was a bit of awkward tension as he shook Jason's hand. But then I remembered Jason *did* ask me out to TNO so...

I smiled awkwardly. "Where are my manners? Why don't you two come inside for a drink? And we can sit and catch up for a while."

"Sounds great," Henna replied. Jason nodded bashfully.

"I, er, I'll just go get started on chores. You guys go on without me. I'm sure you'd like some alone time with your friends anyway." He sounded friendly, but I could see there was hurt in his eyes as he turned and walked away.

I led Henna and Jason inside the farmhouse. I sat on Maxwell's recliner and invited them to sit on the couch. Henna plunked down with a huff. Jason came over to me first and handed me a bag.

"My purse!" I peered inside and found all of my belongings from the night of the party. "Wow. Everything's here."

"Yeah everything is mostly untouched." Henna began. "But, the next day I had Jason turn off your phone. Just in case they're tracking you..." She looked into my eyes. "I know why you ran. And I just want you to know I don't blame you."

"And we haven't told the cops anything," said Jason. "Well, we didn't know where you went anyway so..." His eyes turned to the floor. I felt a twang of guilt for just abandoning him at the party. I'm sure he felt rather stood up.

"I'm sorry guys. I didn't mean to just up and run, but I saw a chance to get away... And, wait, did you say cops?" Panic tickled my nerves.

"Yeah," Henna answered. "Your dad reported you missing the next day." My eyes widened. "But don't worry!" Henna must've seen my face drain of color. "They haven't found anything. No one but us has a clue where you are."

"Oh, thank God." I huffed.

"So, like, are you okay here or what do you want us to do?" Jason asked.

"Oh, er, yes. Guys, really, I'm fine. More than fine, actually. The Lancasters, they really are good people. They pretty much welcomed me with open arms."

"Well, Danny, you're more than welcome to lay low at my place," Jason offered.

I was totally caught off-guard. "Oh, Jason, thanks, but no. I'm okay here, really. They are good people. And, this may sound morbid, but if they were going to kill me I'm sure they would've done it already." Henna giggle hoarsely and her eyes widened. *Okay so that made it sound horrible.*

I then went into a detailed explanation about how much I'd learned from Sam and Maxwell and how well they were treating me. I would've mentioned the parts about Sam and I too, but with Jason in the room, I didn't want to make him nauseous.

"Wow, so you've become quite the country girl?" Henna teased.

"I guess so." I grinned from ear to ear. "To be real honest, I kind of love it here. I have begun to understand why people go to rehabilitation ranches. Something about caring for animals, maybe horses in general, the beautiful landscape every way you turn. It's so healing."

"Amazing. And racehorses. That's so cool." Henna sounded intrigued.

"Yeah, I mean. Don't ask me about their breeding program or anything. I'm a total green-hand at all of this. Sam's the expert of course. But I agree it's very cool, and it seems to have made his family a comfortable life here."

"Hm, yes." Henna eyed me suspiciously. "Sam does

seem like quite the catch." She winked. I knew she would approve if she laid eyes on Sam. I suddenly became hyper aware that Jason was also in the room. He was turning beet red. I felt bad.

Just then, Sam strode through the door.

"Speak of the handsome devil," Henna whispered to me.

"How's the catching up going?" Sam inquired.

"Great," Henna responded. I noticed her lingering eyes on him, but I couldn't blame her.

"Hey, would you guys like to stay for dinner?" I asked.

"Sure!" Henna exclaimed.

"Er, yes. Why not," replied Jason, stiffly.

Sam's voice was a bit strained. "What a great idea." Sam whipped around and began preparing dinner.

I broke the tension. "I completely forgot. Can I get you two something to drink?"

"Sure, a water would be great," Henna replied.

"Soda, if you have it. Doesn't matter what kind," said Jason.

I popped up and got their beverages while Sam was working on a stir fry and rice. I began to set the table for us. Jason and Henna meandered over to sit on the bench seat at the table. When Sam was done he laid out the dishes and we dug in.

Henna broke the silence. "Sam this is really good. How did you learn to be such a good cook?"

"Thank you." Sam looked at her warmly. "My mother taught me."

Henna looked at me and raised her eyebrows, silently signaling this was a desirable quality. I rolled my eyes. Jason saw our brief gestures and his cheeks turned pink.

The rest of dinner was just as awkward. Having Henna

there was great, but the tension crackled between Sam and Jason. Henna kept eyeing Sam like a piece of meat, but that was just Henna's way. I actually found it comforting to know that she saw something in him too. But she had always had a way with men. They flocked to her by the dozens.

When we'd finished eating. Jason stood up. "Well, Henna, I don't want to overstay our welcome. We should probably be heading home." I could tell he just wanted to get out of the awkward agony. I blushed a little realizing two men were actually bristling over plain old me.

"Of course," Henna responded. "You're probably right." She rose from the table too. "It was so nice meeting you, Sam." He rose too as she reached out to shake his hand.

"The pleasure is all mine." Sam replied. Henna's hand lingered. Jealousy finally crept over me. Thankfully, Sam pulled his hand away. Jason was already waiting at the door.

Henna made her way over to me and wrapped me in a tight hug. I breathed her scent in. She may have made me crazy at times, but I still loved her. I squeezed her hard in return. I walked her to the door.

"I'll call you, okay?" I affirmed.

"I'll be looking forward to it." Henna's eyes were wet. "You take care of yourself. Don't hesitate to reach out. Anytime. Middle of the night. You know that, right?"

"Of course I do." I gave her one last squeeze and she and Jason stepped out the door. I waved as she got in her car and began to drive off. I stood in the doorway and watched her taillights disappear into the dim evening. I sighed and shut the door. As I turned around I found Sam leaning against the kitchen wall. He looked at me deeply and his eyes showed his hurt.

"What's wrong?" I ventured.

"Why didn't you tell me?"

"Tell you what?"

"You wrote your friends a letter. Which, don't get me wrong, I understand why you did that. You didn't know us and we didn't know you at that time, but what about now?" I stepped closer and could see his eyes were brimming with tears. He tried to wipe them away. "Why couldn't you have told me now? Don't you trust me?"

I rushed over to him. "It's not that! I didn't think it was a big deal or that it was relevant. Plus, I didn't want you to freak out or be hurt... like you are now. I'm sorry." I wiped the rest of his tears away. "I love you."

I didn't have time to think about what I'd just said as his lips met mine. His hand wrapped into my hair. The ferocity of it sucked the air from my lungs. I regained my breath as he kissed my neck. My heart fluttered in my chest. *I can't believe I just said that.* But, it was true. I turned his chin up and locked my lips with his. Sam scooped me up and started carrying me up the stairs.

My pulse was racing as set me gently on the bed. He unbuttoned his shirt and threw it to the floor. My mouth fell open, mesmerized as I saw his chiseled abs for the first time. A cross necklace dangled against his chest. He watched curiously as I reached out to touch it and then drew my hand down his body. He grinned mischievously. His hand reached for the bottom of my shirt and started to slide it up. This time, his touch didn't bother me, but he froze.

"I'm sorry. I should ask. Is this okay? I mean," he stuttered, "are you okay with this?"

I giggled at his sudden awkwardness. "Yes. I'm more

than okay." I felt my cheeks flush.

With that, Sam pressed his body against mine and I melted into his embrace as we fell back onto the bed.

Chapter 15

The next morning, I opened my eyes and found the bed empty next to me. I was a bit disappointed until the scent of bacon wafted into the room. Then my senses kicked in and I could just make out the sizzling sound downstairs. I threw off the covers, only to remember I was still naked. Scrambling, I snatched up my clothes off the floor and scampered to my room. I picked out fresh clothing and made my way to the bathroom. Looking in the mirror, I found a messy black wad of what used to be my hair. Horrified, I fumbled for my hairbrush and made slow progress through the tangles. Once satisfied, I hastened down the stairs.

I found Sam at the stove. He was humming to himself as he turned the bacon in the pan. I blinked in the bright light of the sun coming through the kitchen windows. I saw he already had a big pile of toast on the table with two kinds of jam. I was making my way to the toast when he heard me.

"She wakes!" He was looking over his shoulder. "After last night, I wasn't sure if you'd wake until noon."

"Oh, you exaggerate." I retorted. "Hey, I was meaning to ask you, what's the significance of your necklace?"

Sam pulled the little gold cross out of his shirt. "This? It was my mother's. She gave it to me just days before she passed. Always wore this old thing. She was strong in her faith. Me, not so much, but I like to wear it to remember her by."

"Awe. That's really sweet." I grabbed a piece of toast and spread some jam on it. Then I hunted for some coffee. Sam had not yet started it, so I grabbed the filter and shoved it into the pot, dumped in the grounds, and filled the water reservoir. I pressed start on the device and turned to Sam.

"So, what kinda service is this? You didn't even start the coffee?" I jibed.

"Oh! Here I am slaving away, making you bacon, eggs, and toast, and sure enough, you find something to complain about!"

"Oh, no. You know what?"

"What?"

"We fight like an old married couple." I made a shocked face. Sam laughed.

I was hovering over the coffee pot when Maxwell burst through the door.

"Hey, kids," he called to us.

"Hi, Dad, how was the trip? We didn't even hear you drive in."

"Was good. Went off without too much trouble. We've got a lot to unload."

"That's good. Breakfast will be ready in a minute. Danny is on coffee control." Sam explained.

I gave a thumbs up.

"Good deal. Wow looks like you two held down the fort pretty well." Maxwell was beaming with pride. Sam and I shot each other a glance.

"Yeah, it went okay." Sam said. He made no mention of Henna or Jason so I decided not to either.

Sam set the food on the table. Maxwell was already sitting. I waited patiently for the coffee to finish up, and then brought the pot with me to the table. Taking up my spot next to Sam, I eagerly filled up my breakfast plate. The bacon was heavenly. I was pleasantly surprised to know that Sam was a decent cook. It was certainly some culture shock for me because I was the singular cook for my father and me. In fact, if I hadn't cooked, I don't know if Bill would've eaten.

Sam and I were wolfing down our breakfast, meanwhile, Maxwell was just sipping on his coffee. He hadn't yet touched his food. Sam and I exchanged glances. We must've both been staring at him, because Maxwell looked up at us and sighed. We were patiently waiting for whatever was on his mind.

"I just can't hide anything from you two, can I?" He wiped a hand down his face. "I wasn't sure how to tell you this, or even if I should, but I can't exactly say nothing now." He paused and took a sip of coffee. "Well, Danny, I saw something that may alarm you, but I don't want you to be scared, okay?" I nodded, but my heart started to pound. I set down my fork and coffee cup. Maxwell continued. "I drove through the city yesterday and I stopped at the bank. There was a missing person's poster on the bank window. It had your face on it."

"Oh, yes. Er, would you just excuse me for a bit?" I got up from the table. I already knew from Henna that I'd been reported missing, but I needed to clear my head for a bit. I didn't wait for a response. I walked out the door and started heading for the barn.

I'm glad neither of them followed me out right away. I quickly saddled up Clarabelle and before I knew it I was flying across the ground. The wind was whipping through my hair. Tears were whipped off my face. However, I began to calm down by the time Clarabelle and I reached the bottom of the hill. I leaned forward as she climbed it with ease. We kept on, weaving through the forest.

When we made it to the little clearing with the stream, Clarabelle automatically slowed to a walk and stopped next to the stream. She leaned her head down for a drink as she puffed. I just sat on her for a moment, gathering myself, not entirely sure what to do. Hopping off of her, I walked over to a stump a few feet away, and sank down. Tears were still making their way down my face. I just didn't know what to do with the information. *What was I supposed to tell these guys to do? What if Bill came for me? Would he hurt me? Would he hurt Sam and Maxwell?* I sobbed. I didn't want anyone to be harmed because of me. And I also didn't want to have to go back to Bill. I wanted to stay at Lancaster Farm.

After a while, I heard horse footfalls coming down the trail. I didn't even bother to look up. Clarabelle was still standing at the water's edge, grazing at the sedge grass. Sam and Charlie came racing into the clearing. Dirt flew as Charlie skidded to a halt. Sam jumped off before Charlie even came to a stop. He ran over to my side.

"Danny! I'm glad you're safe." He hugged me into his chest. I looked up at his face. He looked pale with worry.

"Sorry I ran," I whispered.

"It's okay. I understand. I'm just glad you didn't get hurt." Sam tucked a strand of my hair behind my ear.

"I just... I'm so scared. I don't want anything to happen to you or to Maxwell. You're all I have. And you don't know Bill. He's crazy. I don't know what he'd do." I looked down at my shoes.

Sam squeezed my shoulder. "Hey, don't worry. We know how to protect ourselves out here in the backwoods. We'll keep you safe. Besides, he doesn't even know where you are."

"I know. But that doesn't make me any less terrified of him. He had complete control over me for years. You don't understand how awful it was." I shuddered. "I was in constant fear. Everything I said or did was under continuous surveillance and scrutiny. Any moment, I could've triggered him. He went absolutely off the rails when he found out about my first boyfriend. He goes wild at the drop of a pin." Sam stood up and offered me a hand.

"It doesn't have to be like that, you know," he said.

"Like what?" I inquired.

"Him having control over you. You're a strong woman. You could stand up to him." Sam's voice was full of pride.

"Yeah, right. I'm like a tiny ant to him. Easily squashed." I crossed my arms in defeat.

"No, that's not true. At least not anymore." Sam lifted my chin. He looked thoughtful. "I have an idea."

"Oh, no, not another one of those. Don't hurt yourself," I teased through my tears.

"Hey, I'm serious." His eyes pleaded.

"Okay, what's your big idea?" I wiped my eyes.

"What if I taught you to shoot? We have our own range in the back. It'd be empowering. You'd be able to protect yourself, not just from your father, but from any intruder or attacker." His eyebrows raised hopefully. "I'd even let you use my guns."

"Oh, my, not your precious guns!" I teased, but then I pondered for a moment. I was a bit terrified at the thought, but exhilarated. "Actually, I do kinda like that idea."

"Great. How about in a few days I take you out to practice? We have a lot of hay to unload today, if you're still up for it."

"Of course," I said as Sam helped me up. "Let's get to it."

Chapter 16

Sam led me down the stairs into the basement. They were rickety, wooden steps that creaked under our weight. The basement was dark and cool, and smelled a little musty. Sam led the way toward the middle of the room and pulled a chain for some light. It was still pretty dim.

Home built shelves were all around us, each with its own set of random items. Some larger things were also scattered on the floor, including several large dressers and cabinets. There was also a tool bench against a wall with some rusty tools hanging from its pegs. Sam walked toward the metal safe standing next to it. He turned the mechanism and opened it up.

Inside the safe were about ten guns all standing neatly in their own nook in the structure. There were also two shelves; one for some ammunition and the other appeared to have several smaller gun cases on it. Sam grabbed two guns from the bottom and one from the top. Then he sorted through the ammunition containers, grabbing the ones that corresponded to the guns he'd picked out. Satisfied, he handed me the ammo and the small gun case to carry upstairs. He grabbed the other two long barreled guns and started up the stairs. I trailed after.

My palms were a bit clammy. I was nervous for my first time shooting a gun. In fact, it was my first time ever being this close in proximity to one. I had only ever seen them in movies. It was a possibility, though, that Bill could own one. Having never ventured into his bedroom, I never knew. However, I prayed that he did not. That was the last thing a man like him should have.

Sam loaded the guns into the old farm truck and we climbed into the cab. We drove down the gravel path between the pastures, then followed a wider road to the left. The path took us along a field edge and skirted the bottom of a small mountain. Bumping along the trail, we traveled around to the back side. We came upon a sandy patch. The sand cascaded from halfway down the mountain's side and flowed to the bottom. Sam stopped the truck there.

We hopped out and he flopped the tailgate down. Then he grabbed one of the long cases and popped the latches open.

"This was my grandfather's shotgun. It's a twelve gauge. Pretty standard." Sam cracked it open and put in two shells. "Here's a pair of earmuffs to deafen the sound a bit." He handed me orange muffs and I slipped them over my ears. His voice was a bit muffled as he continued talking. "Watch me fire a few rounds into that barrel over yonder. Then, you can give it a try."

Sam stepped a few paces away and raised the gun to his shoulder. He aimed down the barrel and pulled the trigger. *Bang!* I jumped. I heard the round make a "ting" sound as it hit the plastic barrel. Again, Sam raised the barrel and steadied himself as he looked down the sights. He squeezed the trigger. *Bang!* This time I only flinched a little. He opened the gun and popped out the shell casings then looked over at me. I slid my earmuffs to my neck.

"That wasn't too bad, was it?" Sam looked at me hopefully.

"No, it wasn't. I jumped pretty hard at the first one, but the second time I just flinched. I have to admit, though, I'm pretty nervous to even touch that thing."

"That's alright. I don't expect you to be an expert right off the bat. Plus, I'll be right beside you every step of the way." He smiled warmly.

He guided me to stand in a straight line with the plastic barrel on the other side. Then he handed me the gun. I gripped it with shaking hands. The gun was a bit heavier than I expected. He helped me place it against my shoulder.

"Now, this gun has what's called open sights. It's these two notches." He pointed to the little bead of metal and then its counterpart notch on the tip of the gun. "If you line up this front part into the groove on the end, and then line that up onto whatever you want to hit, you should, in theory, be spot on." I looked at him with bewildered eyes. "Don't worry about being perfect the first time. Just do your best."

"I'll try." I lifted the gun. Sam stood right behind me, his arm wrapped around to guide my right hand. He led my finger to the trigger.

"If you want a steady hand, just make sure to squeeze the trigger, not pull. You want a slow action, not a quick jerk. Take a breath as you look down the sight at your target. Relax. When you're good and ready, go ahead and shoot. I'll be right next to you. Keep in mind, the gun will have some kickback. Don't be scared." I nodded.

Looking down the sights, I examined my target. The barrel was about my size, so I prayed I wouldn't make a huge fool of myself by missing. I lined up the sights as best as I could. I took a deep breath in, filling my lungs.

My breath came out shakily. Slowly, my index finger squeezed the trigger. The gun reacted and the butt of it was thrust into my shoulder. I stumbled back into Sam.

"Hey, not bad!" Sam exclaimed. "I saw dirt flying behind the barrel and I heard it, so you must've hit it."

"Thank God. I was shaking so bad."

"You didn't have your eyes shut, did you?" Sam teased.

"No! I was using the sights just like you told me!"

"Good job. But that's enough for the shotgun. Not much use for that around here. Let's have you try the rifle next." Sam grabbed the shotgun from me and wandered over to the truck to retrieve the rifle. He opened a case and pulled out a long-barreled gun with gold accents. It was pretty, with fancy engraving along the sides.

"This one's mine. It's a .30-30. I mostly use it for hunting, but if I venture out for an overnight trail ride, I pack this or the handgun with me for safety." He handed it to me. It had about the same weight as the shotgun.

"Now, here're two bullets." He handed me two long bullets. "They go in on this side." Sam helped me push them into the hole on the side of the gun. "Pull down the lever." He guided my hand as we pulled the lever down and then back up together. "You have a round loaded in the chamber. If you were to pull the trigger right now, it would fire. So, you can choose to turn on the safety, which is right here." Sam pointed to a little nubbin on the side. "Or you can put your thumb on the hammer and gently squeeze the trigger to slowly let the hammer up." He helped me slowly guide the hammer up. "Now all you'd have to do to fire is pull back the hammer and switch off the safety. But another important note, is that this gun has a scope on it, as you can see." He gestured to the top of the gun. "When you have the gun butt up to your shoulder, you can then look into the scope and you'll see crosshairs. Go ahead and take a look."

I raised the gun to my shoulder and peered into the scope. It was a bit blurry, but I could make out two lines, one vertical and the other horizontal.

"If you line up where they cross, on the point you wish to shoot on your target, you should hit your mark. Of course, other things are at play — like, if your sight is adjusted right and operator error, but in theory you'd hit it. Go ahead and give it a try."

I nodded and raised up the rifle. The butt was secured against my shoulder. I adjusted my feet shoulder width apart and one slightly behind the other to have a more stable stance. Still shaking a little, I did my best to look into the scope and line up my shot. I was going for the middle of the barrel. My thumb fumbled a bit for the hammer, but I reached it and pulled it down. Then flicked off the safety. My lungs drew air in, and then slowly out. I squeezed the trigger. Bang! The gun pushed into my shoulder, but this time I didn't stumble back.

"Holy crap! I think you hit it again!" I hoped I had hit it. That was the point at least. "Keep your gun pointed at the ground then, while I go take a look." Sam skipped off to look at the barrel. He tipped it toward the sunlight to get a good look. "Wow, I can't believe it." He looked back at me. "So, where were you aiming?"

My cheeks flushed. *Oh no, did I miss that miserably?* "I aimed for dead center as best as I could," I shouted. "Why?"

"Well, 'cause you hit the outer ring of the target... unbelievable." Sam shook his head in disbelief. "I hope it's beginner's luck or you'll be showing me up in no time. Here, I'll make a mark by this one, so we can tell where you hit with the next one." He got out his pocket knife and scratched into the barrel.

Sam made it back to stand behind me. "Okay, now, to shoot again, you wanna lever your second round into the barrel. So, quickly pull the lever down and then back up. It'll also kick your other casing out."

I put my hand through the lever, pulled it down, and slammed it back up. The used shell flew up and out to the side, landing on the sandy ground somewhere to my right. I raised the rifle again and lined up my shot. Breathe in. Breathe out. Crosshairs, right on the hole from my last shot. I pulled the trigger, only flinching a little. Levering out the used shell, I handed the gun to Sam and ran to the barrel myself. Crouched down in front of it, I could see where Sam had written my initials next to my first shot, then I saw my second shot, just a few inches up and to the right of the first. My heart fluttered. A big smile spread across my face. *I think I just found my new hobby.*

"I nailed it again!" I shouted with glee, jumping up. "Either you're a good teacher, or I'm a natural." I stuck my chest out proudly as I walked back to him.

"Well, are you ready to try this one out, Sharpshooter?" He was holding out a revolver pistol.

"Absolutely." I grabbed the handle of the pistol. It was surprisingly heavy for its size and I nearly dropped it. Sam grinned and handed me six bullets.

"Push this." He pointed to an odd-looking button. "It releases the cylinder, so you can load it." I pushed the release and the gun popped open to reveal the cylinder with six open holes. "Place the bullets in each one. Then push the cylinder back in place." I followed his instructions and placed each of the rounds, then pushed the cylinder back shut. "Let's move a little closer to the barrel so you can get a better shot." We walked up to the barrel until we were about fifteen feet away. I could easily make out the previous bullet holes. Sam continued, "Now, this works pretty much the same as the rifle in terms of hammer and trigger. When you're ready to fire, pull back the hammer and then squeeze the trigger, and off she goes. As for your grip, put your right hand on the handle and then wrap your left hand around that for support." He guided my hands in place. "Whenever you're ready, go ahead, just keep in mind that this one does have kickback, but the force will carry through your arms rather than your shoulder. Your arms might wanna jerk upwards. Just be careful."

"Yes, coach. Thank you, coach. I'll be careful." I made a face at him and then refocused on my target.

I noticed that this gun had the open sights, too, so I did my best to look down the short barrel of the gun and line them up on the center of the target. I squeezed the trigger and the gun went off, sending a shockwave through my arms. It was louder than the others and my ears rang, even though I was wearing my muffs. However, the power in my hands was exhilarating. Adrenaline pulsed through my body. I had never felt so invincible in my life.

"You can keep going and shoot all five more. Just pull the hammer back again," Sam shouted.

"Okay!" I replied and pulled back the hammer. Steadying myself, I lined up my shot and pulled the trigger, again and again, until I ran out of rounds. *Bang! Bang! Bang! Bang! Bang!* I pointed the barrel toward the earth as I handed it off to Sam. He emptied the cylinder and set it back on the tailgate on its case.

"Let's go check out that barrel!" He sounded just as excited as I felt. We trotted off to investigate.

Three out of my six shots made the central portion of the barrel. One more grazed the outside and another hit the top. One was unaccounted for; most likely it had missed entirely. Still, I was quite pleased with myself.

"Remind me not to piss you off." Sam joked as he examined my shots.

"Yeah, not too shabby, am I?" I smiled widely. Sam put an arm around me as we walked back to the truck.

"Not at all. In fact, I think you'll make for an excellent marksman with a little more practice. But it also looks like I'll have to keep practicing, too, if I wanna keep up with the likes of you." He elbowed me as we approached the tailgate. I giggled proudly.

I assisted Sam in putting the guns back in their cases, then we hopped back into the truck.

"Do you feel safer now?" Sam asked as we bounced along the trail towards the farm.

"Actually, yes. A lot. I can finally protect myself."

"Good." Sam squeezed my hand. "I'm glad you won't have to live in fear anymore. If anything, it's others that should fear you, now. I mean, with that aim." He smirked.

"You're darn right they should," I replied triumphantly. Never before had I felt so safe from the threats of life. I could finally defend myself and that power felt so good. I would be truly free of my father's vice grip on my life and on my mind. Sam was right. I was now a force to be reckoned with.

Chapter 17

I just got off the phone with Henna, telling her about my experience with target shooting, when the phone rang right next to my head. I jumped. I stepped away as Maxwell set down his coffee cup and strode over to answer it. A big smile spread across his face.

"Amanda!" he exclaimed. "It's so good to hear from you, sweetheart. How is everything?" He paused to hear her reply. Sam and I gave each other curious glances.

"That's great, dear!" Maxwell continued. "We certainly will be excitedly waiting. See you soon, sweetie." Maxwell returned the phone to its hook. "Amanda's coming to visit for the weekend. Should get here in time for dinner." His voice was filled with joy.

"Cool. That'll be nice," Sam said. He turned to me. "You'll like her a lot, Danny. I can't wait for her to meet you!"

"Ha-ha, yeah, me neither!" My voice held a nervous quaver. *I hope she approves of me, but what if she hates me? Or what if we can't get along?*

∞∞∞

I followed Sam out to the barn and we began to let out the horses for the day. It was a beautiful, sunny, early fall day. There was a cool breeze gently rustling my hair as we sent the horses to pasture. We went back into the barn to muck out some stalls. I grabbed the tools as Sam went to find the wheelbarrow. We met back at the first set of stalls. Sam set the wheelbarrow on the alley in between the first set. I handed him his shovel.

We got down to work on mucking. Sam dumped a shovel full into the wheelbarrow. "It'll be so nice for you to finally meet her. I'm so excited."

"Yeah, it'll be cool, but why are you so jacked up about it?"

"Well, I just hope she'll really like you. She couldn't really stand any of my past girlfriends and, of course, especially not Brittany. Never got along. Amanda liked working with the horses, being outdoors, and getting her hands dirty. Brittany didn't. Not that Amanda doesn't like to dress up, she just wasn't into that cliquey, gossipy crowd. That's not her thing, but that's also why I think you two'll get along swimmingly."

"Oh, yeah, I suppose it'd be nice to have a girl to talk to." I was still nervous to meet Amanda. I didn't know what she already knew about me and what she would think of me freeloading off of, not only her brother and father, but also all of her things and her bedroom. I felt so guilty. And if Sam had talked to her about me, what if I didn't live up to her expectations?

Sam leaned on his shovel in the stall across the alley. "I think I also want her approval... at least a little bit." He looked down at his shoes. "Since my mom passed, Amanda kinda took on that maternal role in our family. Her opinions are important to me. It gives me an idea of what Mom would've thought. And I truly wish she could've met you."

I dumped a shovel into the wheelbarrow and stood for a moment, looking at Sam's troubled face. "It'll be great to meet her. I don't mean to be rude about it. Sorry if I was. I'm just nervous. I really wanna make a good impression. But, I don't know if I will. What if she thinks I'm just a freeloading creep?"

Sam looked up at me, surprised. "She won't think you're a freeloading creep! I already told her as much as she needed to know about why you're here. She knows the circumstances that brought you here. She knows where you came from and she knows to keep her mouth shut about it. She also knows how much I've grown to care about you." His eyes drifted to the floor and his cheeks flushed.

"That helps a little bit, but I hope you haven't put me on too high of a pedestal either. Now, what if I end up disappointing her—"

"You won't disappoint her." He sounded so confident. "She'll like you, I'm sure. Have a little faith in yourself." Sam reached out and squeezed my shoulder and then got back to work.

I turned and worked on my stall too. My mind was a flurry of visions of what the night would bring. *What if I didn't fit into their family? Is she going to even like me? What if she or her husband turns me in? What if she is upset about me using her stuff?*

∞∞∞

Later that evening, I cleaned up after barn chores and then helped Maxwell make dinner. I assisted Sam in setting the table. We had just placed the last dish when ve-

119

hicle headlights made their way across the kitchen wall. My heart skipped a beat. Nerves kicking in full force, I became jittery. Sam and Maxwell went to the door as I stood by the dining table and waited. They rushed outside to help Mark and Amanda unload their luggage. Sam was the first one back through the door with a suitcase. He set it down at the bottom of the stairs as Maxwell came back in. He was followed by a slender, dark haired man, and then a tall, blonde woman with an amazing physique. She shut the door. Sam came to stand by my side. The color drained from my face and my palms began to sweat.

Chucking her bags down by the door, the blonde woman turned to me. "You must be Danny! I've heard so much about you!" Amanda came right over and threw her arms around me. I didn't even know what to do.

"Yes, this is my girlfriend, Danny. Danny, the one with the awkward death grip on you is my sister, Amanda." Sam's voice was teasing.

Amanda let me go. "Nice to meet you, Amanda," I said sheepishly.

"Likewise, Danny." Amanda smiled warmly. She was looking at me with big, beautiful, blue eyes. Her blonde hair falling down her shoulders in perfect, waterfall curls. Her t-shirt and yoga pants were fitted to her outstanding form. I felt like an ugly bridge troll standing next to her.

"I hope you've heard all good things about me," I said.

"Mostly, yes. Sam's texts wouldn't stop raving about the lovely girl he met." Amanda's eyes were understanding. "I nearly forgot!" Amanda's arm swung out wildly toward her husband. "Danny, this is my husband, Mark." Mark nodded.

Sam walked toward the table. "Who's hungry? I know I brought my appetite." He plunked down in his usual spot.

"Do you ever *not* have an appetite?" Amanda teased. Sam turned around and stuck his tongue out at her.

I was making my way to sit by Sam and nearly collided with Amanda. My face turned hot as I realized that must've been her usual spot.

"I'm sorry. Go ahead. I can sit next to Dad." She made her way around the table across from me while I took up my spot by Sam. Mark sat in the chair that was pulled up on the end.

Maxwell began serving everyone the chicken he had baked and we all dug into the sides; green beans, mashed potatoes and gravy, and buttery corn. It smelled and looked heavenly.

"Wow, this is great, Dad!" Amanda chimed in. "You've become quite the cook!"

"Thanks, sweetheart." Maxwell beamed. "So, how's everything going at the clinic?"

Mark answered, "It's been really good. Steady client load."

"Yeah, it's picked up a bit I'd say. It's going really well," Amanda said. "We hired another receptionist to work with me and she's just a blast to work with. How're things here? How's your new farm hand doing?" Amanda winked at me.

"She's awesome," Sam replied. "We've sold several horses over the last month, so that brought in some cash flow. Danny and I have been working with the horses together, especially two youngsters, Vera and Lightning. And Danny's a fast learner, so she's been a big asset. Starting to fill your shoes, that's for sure." Sam looked at me with pride filled eyes.

"Wow. Impressive. Oh, and speaking of filling my shoes, I just wanted you to know, Danny, that it really is totally fine that you're using my stuff. It was just things I left behind from my college days so, as far as I'm concerned, you can just keep them. It's no biggie." She gave me a kind, understanding smile. My cheeks flushed in embarrassment.

"Thanks," I peeped out.

"Also, related to that topic, what room should Mark and I stay in this weekend?" Amanda asked.

"Why don't you stay in your old room," Sam replied, "and Danny can stay in mine." My heart skipped and then sank as Sam continued. "I'll just take the couch."

I looked at Amanda. "I'll grab some of my things out of your room and toss them into Sam's."

"Sounds great!" She gave me a warm smile.

Maxwell and Mark stood up and cleared the table. Amanda and Sam went to bring their luggage upstairs. I scurried after them. Sam grabbed several bags and Amanda took her large suitcase.

I opened the bedroom door for them and they plopped the luggage down onto the bed. My eyes widened as I saw a few stray clothes of mine scattered on the floor. Quickly, I picked up the clothes and chucked them into a basket. Then, I grabbed several different articles of clothing to bring to Sam's room for the night. I dumped them onto Sam's bed. Scanning the room, I worked on finding a place for my stuff. Across the hall, I could just barely make out Amanda and Sam's conversation.

"Ok, spill it," Amanda demanded giddily. "How're things really going with her?"

"Well." I could hear a little embarrassment in Sam's

voice. "She's kind of unbelievable," Sam replied. "Smart, caring, funny, and even though she's from the city, she's never stopped impressing me with how well she works on this farm." He paused. "She's been here for only a few months, but... it feels like I've known her forever." Sam's tone was serious. I found myself leaning against the half-closed door, straining to listen in.

"That's kinda what it was like for Mark and I," Amanda began. "When we met in college, he was a stranger to me, but we had this instant connection." She snapped her fingers. "I always wondered how it could be possible to feel so deeply so quickly, and to feel like you've known each other forever, in only a few short days."

"That's exactly what it's like!" Sam exclaimed.

"I completely get it. I was like you, too. But, don't put too much pressure on yourselves. Just let it happen, however it plays out. It's like the old adage, 'whatever will be, will be.' You'll know what's right." I heard her gently pat Sam. "And, don't worry about the timing. I've seen couples married for years that only knew each other for a few months, and I've seen people that've been dating for ages and their marriage lasted less than a year. You can't judge a relationship based on time alone. So, don't trouble yourself over it."

"Thanks. You don't know how much your words mean to me."

"I think I might have an idea." Amanda paused. "But truly, I'm so happy for you, Sammy. She does seem lovely and she clearly fits in with you and Dad so well. I can't wait to get to know her over the rest of the weekend." Amanda's voice grew sad as she continued. "It's been a long time since I've had a gal pal to hang out with here on the farm..." Amanda trailed off.

"Yeah, I know. I miss her too." Sam replied. "But, Danny reminds me of Mom a lot. And they both started out as city girls." Sam chortled a little. "But... I'm glad you like her so far. Maybe you two could go on a short ride together?" Sam questioned. I got a little nervous. *Alone time with Amanda?*

"That's a great idea!" She exclaimed.

"You can borrow Charlie if you wanna. Danny's been riding Clarabelle."

"Awe, good old Clarabelle. Gosh, Mom loved that horse. And when I pictured a wife for you, Sam, I always thought of someone like Mom. Strong, loving, witty, dedicated..." Amanda replied.

"Danny is definitely all those things..." Sam trailed off.

Amanda's voice turned bright. "Well, then, I don't know what you're so worried about anymore. You should reconsider getting married, Sam."

As I heard that I coughed and nearly choked. They both immediately rushed in to my rescue.

Sam looked concerned. "Are you okay?"

"Yeah, I just coughed. It's no big deal."

"Good," Amanda said, patting me on the shoulder. "Let's go and get some hot cocoa and watch some TV. Then, I think it'll be high time for bed." We followed her toward the stairs.

Amanda handed me a steaming mug of hot chocolate and I snuggled into the couch next to Sam. Amanda was on my other side. Maxwell was in his chair and Mark had pulled up another wooden rocker. I wrapped my hands around my warm mug and buried my head into Sam's shoulder.

My eyes wandered around the room at the others. I couldn't help but wonder what it would have been like if I had grown up in a family like theirs; if I would have turned out any differently, or if we are predestined to be the person we are. Either way, I'd gladly suffer through it all over again, knowing that this is where I would end up now, feeling safe and loved with kind-hearted people. My faith in humanity had been restored.

Chapter 18

I watched as Amanda's flowing, blonde hair glistened in the morning sunshine. The air was crisp as the three of us headed to the barn. Sam and Amanda were walking side by side as I trailed after. Amanda threw open the barn door. She didn't seem to miss a beat and got right to work, grabbing a few lead ropes off the hooks. I followed suit. Without saying a word to each other, her and I started by taking two horses at a time to their paddocks while Sam got started with the wheelbarrow. Amanda spoke to me as we took out the first set of horses.

"So, how do you like it here?"

I glanced around at the horses and back at the barn where Sam was. "I love it. It's everything I never knew I needed." A smile broke across my face. Amanda grinned too.

"I hear ya." She looked around and took in a deep breath. "There's just something about a place like this that soothes the soul."

"That's for sure," I responded.

Amanda stumbled over her next words. "Yeah, I kinda heard about you a bit. From Sam, of course. You had it pretty rough back in the city?" She opened the gate and we let the horses in.

"Um, yeah. I suppose so. I mean... I guess that's pretty much why I ran away." I looked down at the ground while she shut the gate.

"That's too bad. Sam mentioned your dad has kind of a mean streak. And you lost your mom when you were young, too. That must've been tough for you."

"It was." I looked over at her and met her kind eyes. "And mean streak is an understatement." Amanda's eyes grew curious as we walked back to the barn.

"So... it's true then? That he hit you, I mean?"

My voice was matter of fact. "Unfortunately, yes. More times than I can count... I just couldn't take living in fear anymore... so I ran."

"That must've taken a lot of courage." Her words surprised me.

I half giggled. "You have no idea. It's the hardest thing I've ever done. And even though Sam and Max have helped me overcome a lot, to be honest, I'm still a little scared."

Amanda patted my shoulder. "You have every right to be. I can't even imagine what you went through for all those years. I'm so glad you found your way here. You were just what these boys needed." I grinned. She continued. "My dad told me last night that the house feels whole once more with you in it." Amanda beamed and squeezed me around the shoulders as we walked back into the barn. "And I guess Sam thinks you're pretty cool, too," Her mocking voice was loud enough for Sam to hear.

Sam's head peeked around the corner of a stall door and he just smiled and rolled his eyes at her. Amanda grabbed Sam's full wheelbarrow and went to dump it while I took several more horses. It was awesome to see how well Amanda fit right in with the farm chores, even though she had not worked on the farm for quite some time. Maybe it's like riding a bike; you never forget.

It also amazed me how I was no longer afraid of the giant horses. I was proud of myself for coming this far. Apparently, I fit in pretty well, too. Confidently, I strode out of the barn, leading three horses in tow. I took in a deep breath. *Gosh, it feels good to be here. Fresh air, cool breeze, breathtaking beauty all around me. This is the life!*

∞∞∞

As Sam took out the last wheelbarrow load, Amanda came to stand next to me, leaning on her pitchfork. She wiped her brow on her flannel shirt. Her blonde hair now damp. Sweat dripped down my neck too.

"Whew, glad we're done with that." Amanda let out a puff. "Now I get to see how far you two have come with Vera and Lightning." She sounded excited.

"Well, you mean how far Sam has come. I only helped him a—"

Amanda cut me off. "Nonsense! He said you've put in some major work on them, especially with Vera! Don't sell yourself too short." And before I could say any more, she gave me a sharp pat on the back and walked away. My mouth was still agape. Amanda sure was something else. I stood there, dumbfounded for a moment, until Sam walked back in and plopped some ropes into my hands.

"Here," he said, "why don't you go get Vera and Lightning and I'll prep the tack here quick."

I looked down at the ropes. "Okay." I obediently followed directions and went on my merry way to grab the horses.

On my way, I planned out my approach. When I entered their pasture, I draped one of the leads over the fence. I approached Vera first, since, even after all this time, she was still easier to catch. I called to her and slowly walked over. She turned toward me. We met each other halfway and she snuffled in my pockets.

"Oops, sorry, Vera. I forgot your treats." I had been bringing treats with me to help coax her into coming when called. "Next time, I promise. And probably after training today." I chattered away to her as we walked back toward the fence. I tied her loosely to the fence line, so I could go fetch Lightning.

He was standing toward the back of the paddock, not even paying me any attention. His tail was gently swishing away the last of the flies before the cold weather set in. I skirted around behind him and came at him from an angle. His ears finally twitched in my direction and he picked his head up from the grass he had been nibbling. I spoke softly to him as I carefully approached. His nostrils flared a little, but he stood there for me. Gently, I slipped the halter over his muzzle and then over his soft, pointed ears. I led the way back toward Vera. After untying her, the three of us set off toward the barn to get tacked up.

Sam took Lightning and I tacked up Vera. Amanda was leaning against a barn post watching us. I swung the heavy, leather saddle up onto Vera's back. It creaked as I wiggled it into the perfect position. Then, I reached under her and grabbed the other end of the cinch. I patted Vera's shoulder as I walked around the front of her and took the bridle off its hook. Smoothly, I removed her halter and slipped the bridle over her nose and ears. Next, I fastened her throat latch. She stood calmly for me. Finally, I threw the reins over the saddle horn and did one final adjustment on the cinch to make sure it was fit for riding. While I was working, I felt Amanda's gaze burning into me. It felt like I was being assessed. However, when I looked over at her leaning against the post, her expression was nothing short of pleased.

Sam finished up saddling Lightning just before I finished with Vera, so he was already headed out the door. I followed behind him. Amanda brought up the rear. Swiftly, we made it to the training arena. The sand sparkled in the sunlight. Sam had set up some poles for us to practice agility by zigzagging through them. I stepped into the stirrup, swung my other leg over, and sat into the saddle on Vera. We began warming up by walking briskly around the arena. Lightning and Sam fell into step along side of us. Amanda took up a position in the center of the arena.

The sand of the arena gritted under their hooves and the breeze swept Vera's mane gently across her neck. I gave her a gentle pat. She and I had bonded over the last several months and I'd learned much on horsemanship from working with her. Sam did most of the groundbreaking work, but I was now able to ride her fairly confidently. After making several rounds of the arena, I told Vera to trot and gave her flanks a tap with my heels. She instantly responded, and we started on a bouncy trot. I began to post so I didn't bounce right out of the saddle.

Sam called to me. "Danny, you can take Vera through the poles while I run Lightning a bit."

"Okay!" I called back and turned Vera toward the six-foot, white poles Sam had set up for us. I slowed her to a walk as we approached the start. I asked her to walk and we took them slowly, weaving in and out. She completed it with ease. We walked them several more times.

It was so calming riding slowly on a horse. Feeling their breath. The smell of the leather. The jingle of the metal parts and the rocking motion of their hips. I couldn't help but love it. Next, I asked her to trot. It was much harder to guide her through the poles without hitting them while at a faster pace. My toes nicked one of the poles and it wobbled. Her shoulder bumped into one too and we almost knocked it over, but I stopped her abruptly and backed her up slowly. Then, we completed it at the trot. I gave her lots of praise after completing it a couple of times. It was so empowering to have an animal of this size respond to my commands so well. My heart was full.

My gaze jerked up and a shot of adrenaline pulsed through my veins as Lightning zoomed past us. *Where was Sam?* My eyes followed Lightning's dust trail toward the opposite end of the large arena and I saw him sitting up on the sand. He seemed fine, so I quickly turned my attention back to Lightning. Amanda leapt forward and swiftly caught his reins and brought him around. Then, she swung with ease up onto his back. Lightning looked a bit shocked that this stranger just wrangled him, and he put up a fuss. However, Amanda held fast and didn't flinch as he tossed his head and bucked up a bit. I trotted Vera over to Sam.

"Are you okay?" I asked.

"Yeah. Got the wind knocked out of me. He got spooked by something and reared up and I just wasn't ready for it." Sam stood up slowly and dusted himself off. There was sand in his tousled, brown hair.

Amanda came riding up to us with Lightning. "Seems like you're having a hard time staying in the saddle." Amanda teased Sam. "Mind if I work with him for a bit?" she asked.

"Be my guest. I could use a minute."

With that, she dug her heels in and made him turn on a dime. They took off toward the other end of the arena, flinging up dust in their wake.

"Wow," I said as I hopped down off of Vera. "Your sister's an amazing rider." She came zipping past us again, around the end of the arena, and flew back toward the other end.

"She is. I wish she would've stayed working here," Sam replied. "I hate to say it, but she was our best trainer. She really knows how to push 'em hard. And for racehorses, you need that." Sam's gaze followed his sister with admiration.

Amanda came blazing past yet again. The dirt flew up off of Lightning's hooves. He was panting hard, but still tossing his head and defiantly fighting her. Despite his angst, she confidently guided him into the turn, switching his lead leg with ease, then switching back again for a figure eight pattern. Wonder filled my eyes. *What an amazing woman.*

"Hey!" Sam called to his sister. "Wanna race me on the track?" he challenged.

She came zooming up with Lightning. "Of course, I do." She turned her attention to me. "Danny, can you get the gates for us?"

"Absolutely," I said with a grin. This was exciting. I couldn't wait to see both of them in action. I scurried over to the gate and unclipped the chain. Sam jumped onto Vera. Amanda, then Sam, rode out and headed down the path to the dirt track. It was so cool they had their very own training track for the racehorses. I still didn't know much about the mechanics of training them for racing, but it was so awesome to watch.

I swung open the gate to the track and the horses eagerly marched in. The sand and gravel crunched under their feet. I was glad it was a cool fall day, so they wouldn't get as sweaty from running. While the riders positioned their horses, I chained the gate once more. Sam had recently begun running them on the track, so they were both waiting, agitated, feet stomping, head tossing, and chomping at their bits. Personally, I loathed running, so to see these animals so eager to race was appalling. I strode up to them and positioned myself at the edge of the track, right next to the fence.

"On my mark!" I shouted. Amanda and Sam got into position, leaning forward and holding back tightly. "Ready." The horses stomped. "Set." Lightning snorted. "Go!" Amanda and Sam simultaneously dug their heels into the horses' flanks and loosened their reins. They both shot off like rockets, dirt flying up behind them. Sam and Vera started to take the lead. They rounded the first turn and Vera stumbled, having to switch leads, but recovered quickly. However, it put her behind Lightning by about a horse-length. Lightning propelled into the next long stretch. He was slowly gaining inches ahead of Vera and Sam. Amanda pushed him harder. Sam was kicking his heels, but Vera couldn't regain the distance on the stretch. Amanda rounded the second bend with ease. They were headed back toward me. Lightning's nostrils flared. I could see the sweat on his chest. Amanda's gaze burned toward the finish line. Sam was just now rounding the corner. Lightning came blazing up to me, and I felt the wind gust as he blew past me.

"Yahoo!" Amanda shouted as she pulled back on the reins. Lightning slowed to a halt. Sam crossed the finish line with Vera, both of them looking defeated.

He pulled Vera into a halt. "Nice win," he called to Amanda. "That's the fastest I've ever seen him go." Sam patted Vera's shoulder.

"You guys, that was amazing!" I gushed. The horses were still panting heavily.

Amanda pet Lightning's neck. "Yeah, that was a rush. Haven't run a horse in a while. Not since last Thanksgiving. Let's cool them down for a bit." She and Sam began to walk the horses around the track. Letting their muscles stretch back out and relax before we put them back for the day.

When they were thoroughly cooled off, I opened the gate for them, so we could bring the horses back in. Sam waited for me and scooted forward in the saddle, so I could swing up to sit behind him. I wrapped my arms around his strong waist. Lightning and Amanda were in front of us, so I slipped a hand up Sam's shirt. He was sweaty, but I didn't mind. I could feel the definition of his abs. He glanced over his shoulder and grinned at me.

I hopped off when we reached the barn. While Sam and Amanda got off their steeds, I swung open the barn door. They lead their respective horses inside. Amanda began untacking Lightning, so I stood and watched.

"Nice riding out there," Sam declared. Amanda brushed him off.

"That was nothing. Give me a week to prepare and you'd be majorly eating my dust." Amanda lifted the saddle off and hung it on its peg. She then grabbed some brushes, one for her and one for Sam. They brushed the sweat and dirt off their horses. Amanda led Lightning to the wash stall and sprayed him down. Sam followed suit. Lightning's whole body shook as he tried to shake the water from his pelt. We all got sprayed.

"Lightning!" Sam exclaimed.

Sam took Lightning and Vera and began walking them back to their pasture. Amanda strode over to me.

"Hey, I was thinking we could go for a short ride this evening. Just the two of us." Amanda's eyes were hopeful.

"I'd like that." I figured it would be a good opportunity for me to get to know her. I glanced over her shoulder at Sam. *Especially if I was ever to become part of their family.*

"Awesome!" A big smile broke across Amanda's face. She draped an arm casually around my shoulders. "Let's go in for some lunch." I grinned back, and we started off toward the porch.

Chapter 19

Sam pushed me up against the back wall of the tack stall. His breath was hot in my ear as he placed kisses down my neck. Chills spiraled down my spine. His lips made their way to my collarbone and then back up again. I squealed in delight.

"Amanda is gonna be here any minute! We're supposed to be getting tacked up!" I whispered.

"I don't care," Sam breathed back, and he ran a hand up into my hair. His lips pressed into mine and our breathing became heavy. He put an arm around the small of my back and drew me in closer. My hand ran under his shirt to feel the washboard of abs. He giggled at my soft touch. I grinned. Then, I grabbed him and drew him in for a passionate kiss.

Just then, the barn doors on the other end burst open and I shoved Sam away from me like he had the plague. My cheeks flushed hard. Sam walked out of the stall pretending like nothing happened and I grabbed my saddle off the rack next to me. Walking casually toward Clarabelle, I swung the saddle onto her back and began to adjust it. Sam was grabbing the wheelbarrow full of muck and was about to take it out. I looked over at Amanda who was eyeing us suspiciously. I averted my gaze quickly back to Clarabelle.

Amanda did not say a word, but she began to grin. Then, she went about her business getting Charlie out of his stall and starting the process of tacking him up for our trail ride. I was very nervous yet excited to be going with her on the trails. Amanda was quite overbearing, but still very fun to be around.

I tightened my rear cinch. Amanda was just adjusting her girth. Pausing, I used the hairband on my wrist to pull my locks out of my face and into a low ponytail. Sam's hands had left it a little bit messy. Amanda tightened her rear cinch and started with the bridle. I did the same. Using my fingers to slip the bit into Clarabelle's mouth, I pulled the rest of it up and around, behind her ears. I left the reins to rest on the horn of the saddle. I wiped my wet saliva covered fingers on my pants and adjusted the throat-latch. I checked the cinch once more to make sure it was tight enough. I did not want to fall off and look like a fool in front of Amanda.

Amanda was just finishing up tacking too. She smiled over at me and walked over to get some saddle bags to attach for the items we'd be bringing on our afternoon trip. I unclipped Clarabelle and walked her outside. I heard the rattle of the empty wheelbarrow as Sam was on his return trip with it. He gave me a quick kiss and proceeded into the barn. Amanda came out with Charlie and walked toward the house. I followed.

"Here," she said, tossing me the reins, "hold him while I get our stuff." Amanda strode into the house. I made small talk with the two horses while we waited. She returned with two canteens and a handful of snacks. "These are for incase we get hungry. Here, take your canteen." I grabbed the jug from her. She stuffed the snacks and her canteen into one saddle bag, then came around and took mine from me, shoving it into the other bag. "Okay, I think we're all set!"

"Awesome! I'm excited!" I exclaimed.

"We'll have some fun. I'll take you on *my* favorite trail. It'll be a little different than the trails you're used to." She mounted Charlie with ease. I scrambled to follow suit, clumsily swinging my leg over in haste. "Ready?" she asked.

"Yup!"

"Let's go!" Amanda said, taking the lead on Charlie. We were headed for the driveway, which puzzled me. I certainly had not ridden on the road before. We made it almost to the end of the driveway when she paused. "Give me one second." Amanda trotted back toward the barn. That's when I saw Sam waiting at the barn door. She leaned down to talk to him. At first, I thought nothing of their conversation, until I noticed they were casting glances back toward me. Then I got a little nervous. Clarabelle must have sensed my unease because she became fidgety. I couldn't make out what they were talking about, but it was definitely something suspicious.

Amanda came trotting back over to me. "Okay, now I'm ready to go." She smiled and, before I could ask her what their conversation was about, she was off. I glanced back toward Sam, but he smiled warmly and waved me off. I waved back, puzzled. *Well, if they wanted me to know I guess they would've told me.*

Amanda led me on the edge of the road. The gravel crunched under the horses' hooves. Trees were half bare as their leaves made their trek to the ground. Fall was among us. I looked left and right and saw open fields. The fall crops had been harvested. Some contained nothing but corn stubble, yet others had yellowed grasses. Amanda and I both had chosen to wear light jackets to break against the chilly breeze. However, the afternoon sun was still shining amidst its bright blue background.

We turned down the next gravel side road, about three miles from our farm. So far, it had been a quiet and peaceful ride, and we hadn't met a single car. We appeared to be on the Johnson's road and, sure enough, we began to approach a white house and red barn. I could just make out the sound of calves lowing in the distance. We had made it nearly to their driveway as I heard a car approaching behind us. I had just peeked over my shoulder as it came barreling toward us. I panicked. I watched as they nearly ran Amanda and Charlie over. They were turning into the Johnson's driveway. They honked as they went past Amanda and then stopped in the drive. The whole time, Amanda never even flinched. I had a small heart attack. The man driving rolled down the window. It was Jeremy Johnson. He smiled up at Amanda.

"Amanda, long time no see!"

"Yes, hello, Jeremy." Amanda replied curtly.

"How've you been? Are you still liking big city living?"

"It's been fine, yes. How's the farm?" Amanda looked like she wanted to crawl under a rock.

"It's doing well. We have some tough times here and there, but it's surviving. It's so nice to see you again. You really look great."

"Thanks, but we should really get moving if we wanna make it back before sundown."

"Oh, gee, I'm sorry. I'll let you two gals get back to it then. Maybe talk to you later. Have a nice ride."

Amanda gave him a nod and we were off again. She picked up the pace this time. I puzzled over what I had just witnessed. Amanda led us several more miles down the gravel road, paused, and looked back over her shoulder, then proceed to cross the road. I followed suit on Clarabelle. We were at the mouth of a county forest trail based on the worn-out wooden sign at the entrance. I pulled up next to Amanda.

"What the heck was that all about?" I asked her.

For the first time, I saw her blush. "We used to date... back in high school. Needless to say, I find it awkward to talk to him. I never *told* him I'd gotten married, but I assumed he'd know. He should know, right? Unless he's kept his head in the sand."

"Yeah, he should know... But that was... interesting," I replied, raising my eyebrows.

"Oh, put a sock in it." Amanda reached over and gave me a playful shove as she rode onward into the forest. I laughed. She felt like family.

Leaves crunched under Clarabelle's hooves. The forest smelled damp and musky. Red, yellow, and brown leaves dotted the trees. As we trekked onward, the occasional withered leaf would flutter to the forest floor where their brethren lay, and moss grew abundantly. Birds chirped overhead, and squirrels chattered in the distance. Amanda remained silent; the quietest I had ever heard her. She probably missed the peacefulness of the farm and the trails after living in the city. It certainly seemed like a different world to me.

We came upon a small stream. There was a footbridge over the water. It looked rickety to me, but Amanda went forward with confidence.

I, on the other hand, was nervous. I gently nudged Clarabelle onward. She clearly knew the trail because she did not need to be persuaded to cross the sketchy bridge. The boards creaked and groaned under our weight. My heart felt like it was in my throat. I swallowed hard and peered down. I had to laugh at myself. The water was only two feet deep. Clarabelle easily stepped back onto the soft forest path.

"You okay? You looked a little nervous there," Amanda jibed.

"Yeah, I'm fine. Just didn't trust the bridge, but Clarabelle did, so we're all good." I gave my trusty steed a pat on the neck.

"Good. We're almost there. Then, we'll hang out for a little while, let the horses rest, and start on our return journey. Hopefully, we'll be back before nightfall."

"Alrighty." Admittedly, I was a bit nervous about riding in the dark. It would be a new experience for me if we did.

Before long, we reached a small clearing, a meadow. Of course, now it was nothing but yellowed grass, fallen leaves, and dead flowers, not that it didn't possess a certain kind of beauty. Amanda headed for a sole, large tree growing in the center of the clearing. She hopped off Charlie and hitched him loosely to a low hanging branch. I climbed off and did the same.

She stepped out into the clearing. "I know it's not much to look at now, but you should see this spot midsummer. It's beautiful." Amanda twirled around, reminiscing on an old memory. "In the hot months, it's filled with every wildflower you can imagine. The whole clearing is filled with color." Amanda skipped over to me and took me by the hand. "And look, down here is the start of the same stream we crossed earlier. It's spring fed. You can see the water bubbling up over here." She led me to the edge of a small pond and we crouched down to watch the water bubble up. I was mesmerized. Amanda's eyes were beaming with childlike excitement and wonder.

She stood up and directed my attention again.

"Many years ago, I cut these stumps, so I'd have a nice place to sit and enjoy this peaceful spot." Amanda plunked down on a tree trunk stool and patted the one next to her. From that spot, you could view the whole clearing. We were right next to the bubbling pond, and we could see the horses and the rest of the meadow.

"I used to come here to do my homework or clear my head. Not that the farm isn't a wonderful place, but this clearing has a special kind of charm. It's like the county's best kept secret, in my opinion. I've never met another person on the forest trail and besides that, this clearing is slightly off the path, so don't tell anyone that I'm breaking the rules."

"Don't worry, I won't." We giggled like children. "But I can definitely see the appeal here. I used to frequent the library and a quaint little park in my neighborhood. They both were just quiet and peaceful. The park even had a fountain. I really enjoyed that spot. Like you, those were the places I did my homework and found a respite from daily life. I could never concentrate at home, for obvious reasons..."

"Yeah, I don't suppose you could."

I continued, "They were my refuge. The park mostly, just because of that fountain. I loved the foliage in the summertime, too. Whoever took care of that place was my hero. Always beautiful. Much like this spot here, I imagine."

We both sat quietly for a moment, pondering. I was brought back to the peaceful times spent in the park like reading on the bench, losing track of time and nearly missing the bus, joking and laughing with Henna as we did our homework. Then, I drifted to the other times;

huddled under the big tree, crying after Bill hit me, or sitting on the bench until the street lights came on because I was too afraid to go home. Those dark thoughts made me shiver. I got up from the stump and walked back to the horses. Digging around in the saddlebags, I found my canteen. The water was still cool. I looked back at Amanda. She was watching the stream. Her eyes looked sad, too, but for different reasons. I grabbed her canteen out as well and returned to her, the grass rustling under my feet. Without saying a word, I handed her the canteen and settled back onto the stump.

Amanda picked her head up. "Sam really loves you, you know. This is the happiest I've seen him in years."

I pondered for a moment. "I had a feeling he did. However, he hasn't said it yet. Which concerns me. And, if I'm being completely candid, if he doesn't say it soon, I'd have no *real* reason to stay here." As much as I loved Lancaster Farm, if Sam couldn't commit to me, I'd be forced to move on with my life. Amanda looked saddened.

"I can understand that. I'd probably do the same. But, like you, he's been through a lot. Try to give him the benefit of the doubt."

"I will." I promised.

"And if it's any consolation," she continued, "I really like you, too."

My heart warmed a bit and we both smiled.

Amanda looked up at the skyline. "It's starting to get dark. We should mount up."

I followed her toward the horses and we hauled ourselves up. Gathering the reins in my hands, I nudged Clarabelle to walk and we followed Amanda once more into the trees.

My thoughts wandered away from the happy moment

I was trying to hold onto, and instead I found myself reminded that, although I haven't seen or heard of Bill in months, he still loomed over my head like a vicious storm cloud. Rather than have this normal life I dreamed of, I still lived almost every day with a little bit of paranoia. *Would he find me? What if I slipped up and gave away my location? Or worse, what if I already had?*

Chapter 20

As we waved off Mark and Amanda as they pulled out of the drive, my thoughts swirled back on what Amanda had said about Sam. *We haven't been together that long. Am I just crazy for worrying about a simple 'I love you?' The way Sam treats me, he definitely has strong feelings for me. Even now with his warm arm wrapped around me tightly, I can feel that connection. But, how long would I have to wait?*

It felt as though the rest of my life hung on those three little words. We had been dating for nearly two months. I had said it multiple times and each time I was met with a loving gesture, but he never actually *said* it. *But, was it really that big of a deal?* I wasn't sure. Two months is hardly a long time and yet, I knew that, with all my heart, I wanted to stay with Sam and make Lancaster Farm my home, forever.

In the last couple of weeks I had even asked Henna to research what schools in the area offered varying degrees in Business Management. I could help Sam run the farm if only I had the technical skills to do it. Maxwell wouldn't live forever and Sam needed someone to run the books.

Sam guided me to the porch swing to sit. It was only mid-morning. The sunlight was licking the tops of the barn and the trees. A warm, gentle breeze rustled my hair.

Sam interrupted my whirlwind of thoughts. "So, what did you think of Amanda and Mark?"

I pondered for a second. "I didn't get much time with Mark, but he was polite... I really like Amanda." I said it almost sadly. I wished she could be my family. If only Sam could get over his past. *I'm not Brittany. I deserve something wonderful like this, right? After all I've been through?*

"I'm so glad to hear." Sam's voice was cheerful. He was clueless of my inner turmoil. He wrapped his strong arm around me and pulled me into his broad chest. I let him. I loved being near him. I breathed in his woodsy scent. He treated me so well. Better than I have ever been treated. Like a princess. I wanted this to last forever. *Amanda said to just give him a little more time*

Chapter 21

I t was late afternoon and the gentle breeze was tickling the pages of the book I was reading. Sitting on the porch swing, I could see the leaves on the trees were just beginning to turn colors. I was looking up from my book as Sam drove in the driveway with the pickup truck. He had just returned from getting groceries in town. He pulled the truck up and put it in park. He hopped out and grabbed a few paper grocery bags out of the cab and also a long, white box, which he tucked under his arm. Sam walked up the porch steps and set the grocery bags down by the door and turned to me, still holding the long, white box.

"So, I have a question for you." I closed my book and looked up at him. "Are you free this evening?" Sam spoke in a half teasing manner. He knew quite well that I was free every evening. I decided to play along.

"Why, yes. It just so happens. Why, pray tell, do you ask?" Now he got really into it.

"Well, Madam, I was hoping that you would accompany me on a date."

"Hm, well, yes, I suppose that would be acceptable." I tried to keep my composure, but I burst out giggling. "Yes, of course, Sam. I'd love to."

He smiled. "Great. And in that case, I have a little something for you." Sam handed me the box. I eyed him suspiciously. Slowly, I undid the white ribbon tied around it and carefully lifted the lid. I gasped. Folded neatly inside was a beautiful, bright red evening gown. It looked expensive. I searched around for a price tag.

"Sam! This is gorgeous! I love it! My God, how much was this?" Sam just grinned.

"You're worth more to me than anything. Don't worry about it."

My eyes watered a little. "Still, you shouldn't have, but this is wonderful. Thank you." I stood up and gave him a kiss.

"I knew it would look beautiful on you tonight." Sam smiled warmly. "But that's not the only thing I got for you." My eyes widened as he reached down into one of the brown paper grocery bags and pulled out a shoebox. He handed it to me, smiling guiltily.

I peered inside. I set down the dress box and opened the lid of the shoebox. Inside was a pair of sparkling, ruby red pumps. My heart skipped a beat.

"Sam they're so pretty!" I squealed. "Thank you!" I gave him another big kiss and wrapped my arms around him.

"You're welcome." He kissed me on the forehead. "Why don't you go ahead and take a shower while I work on putting away groceries. Then, I'll get cleaned up and we can both get dressed and ready to go."

"Okay!" I snatched up the dress, shoes, and my book, and yanked open the house door. Sam grabbed the grocery bags and stepped through. Then I raced up the stairs.

I set the boxes on my bed and took the dress all the way out of its box. Draping it onto the bed, I looked it over. It was beautiful: bright red with an empire waist, "V" neckline, flouncy capped chiffon sleeves, and a skirt with a chiffon layer. Never had I had clothing so fancy in my life. We never had a lot of money, so I was usually dressed drably. Bill seemed to prefer it that way anyway. I was so excited to try everything on.

Scrambling to the bathroom, I turned on the water and jumped into the shower. I washed up as fast as I could. My excited nerves were making me jittery. I couldn't stop smiling. Hopping out of the shower, I heard Sam's footsteps come up the stairs and then head to his room. I got out a brush and combed through my tangled hair, then blow dried it. My black hair was soft and flowy by the time I was done, falling just past my shoulders. I decided to leave it down. I needed to figure out what to do for makeup. It had been eons since I'd worn makeup, it seemed.

I dug into Amanda's small stock of goods and picked out some simple foundation, a light blush, some black mascara, and a bright red lipstick to match my dress and shoes. After applying my final makeup touches, I stuck in my tiny CZ earrings that I'd been wearing when I came to Lancaster Farm. I looked myself over. *Hair? Check. Makeup? Check. Earrings? Check. What was I missing? Oh, perfume!* I rifled through Amanda's cabinet and found a round, purple bottle. I spritzed some on. It had a fruity scent.

Scurrying out of the bathroom, I returned to my room and picked out some undergarments. Then, it was finally time to put on that dress. Giddy with anticipation, I stepped into it and attempted to zip it up. It took some contorting, but I finally got it. Then, I slipped on my shoes. They sparkled in the light. Turning, I looked in the full-length mirror on the back of the door. I took my own breath away. The dress fit like a glove. The flowy gown hem fell just past my knees, drawing your eye to my adorable shoes. The neckline was low, showed just enough, not too much. I looked girly and dainty and I felt like a princess. I loved it.

Exiting my bedroom, I headed for the stairs. Sam was waiting patiently at the bottom of the steps with another tiny box in his hands. He was so handsome, standing there in a suit and a red tie. His mouth fell open a bit as I came down the stairs and met him at the bottom.

"Danny... wow... I mean, you look... amazing," Sam stammered.

"Thank you. You clean up pretty good, too."

"Gee, thanks." He rolled his eyes. "I do have something else for you. Something extra special." He winked and handed me the box. I hesitated, giving him a 'you shouldn't have' look, then took it from him. He was wiggling with anticipation.

My hands were shaking a little as I untied the blue bow. I popped off the lid. Looking inside, my eyes started to water again. A few tears went streaking down my face as I pulled out the necklace. I held the gold cross in my hand. It had been recently outfitted with a brand new, garnet gemstone and it glittered in the light. I looked up at Sam.

"Sam. Oh, my God... it's wonderful. But, I couldn't." More tears came spilling out.

"Nonsense. Here, lemme help you put it on." Sam grabbed it and stepped behind me. He slipped the necklace around my neck as I held my hair to the side. He easily snapped the clasp together. "Wow, it looks perfect. Here, take a look." Sam guided me to the mirror in the hall. The necklace perfectly accentuated my collarbone. But, the sentiment was the most meaningful.

"Oh, Sam," I sobbed.

"Shhh. It's okay. Hey, don't cry. You'll ruin your makeup." He giggled a bit as he carefully dabbed away my tears.

"I don't know what to say except thank you. The whole ensemble is just perfect and beautiful."

"Yes, you are." Sam beamed. I jumped a little as Maxwell spoke. I was so preoccupied with Sam that I hadn't even noticed him standing in the kitchen.

"Awe, you two are so cute. And, Danny, you look just stunning. But, if you wanna make your reservations, I suggest you hit the road, kids. It's nearly five-thirty."

"Thanks," Sam replied. He stuck out his elbow for me. I obliged and slid my arm through, and he led me out the door.

Sam's car was already parked outside and waiting for us. The glossy paint glistened, and I could tell it had been shined up in preparation. Sam opened my door and helped me in. I made sure to tuck my dress in carefully. Then he got into the driver's seat. My fingers absent-mindedly caressed the necklace. My mind wandered off as I tried to guess where we would be going. *Maybe this was the night! What if he asks for my hand?* My heart raced excitedly as Sam put the car in drive. He reached over to hold my hand as we headed out onto the road.

Chapter 22

We pulled into the parking lot of a fancy looking restaurant with an Italian name on the side. Sam got out, and then came around and opened my door for me. He put his arm out for me and we headed inside.

The restaurant was impeccable. We approached the wait staff to check in and then we were guided to our table. They put us in a relatively recluse corner which was okay by me. I wanted the privacy. Sam took up his spot across from me and the waiter took our drink orders and handed us menus.

"Sam, this place is gorgeous. Just look at those chandeliers!" I gestured up toward the ceiling.

"I know. Lovely, isn't it? I think it's a perfect spot for our first 'real' date, don't you?"

"Absolutely. Besides, it's about time you took me on a 'real' date, Mister. We've been together long enough now."

"Ha-ha, true." He laughed nervously. "My bad on that one. Hopefully tonight will make up for being a little behind the eight ball." Sam gazed deep into my eyes and then returned his gaze to his menu. My heart fluttered.

I fondled the necklace as I looked down at my menu. It was overwhelming. There were many items to choose from and most of them were Italian names for the cuisine. The waiter came to take our orders. I decided to do something simple and just went with Alfredo. Sam chose some sort of meaty pasta dish.

We sipped on our beverages. I looked over at Sam. He was so handsome in his well fitted suit and it was sweet how he had coordinated his red tie to match me. In fact, it was a grand gesture that he had gone above and beyond, and got me the dress, shoes, and necklace. My mind was thoroughly blown. *How did I get so lucky?*

"Sam?" I asked tentatively. "Do you think your Mom approves of me wearing her necklace?"

He looked surprised I'd had to ask. "I know she does. I couldn't think of a better way to honor her." He smiled. "What about you, Danny? Do you have anything to remember your mom by?"

I thought for a moment. "No, not really. Bill has kept some of her things like her wedding ring, jewelry, some clothes and stuff, but I was only five when it happened. I barely remember her. I mean, I remember loving her and having fun with her, but picturing her face is so hard." My face scrunched as I tried to imagine what she looked like.

"Yeah, it's hard for me to picture my mom, too. Time seems to fade the images of them away. At least we have the pictures and the feelings. I'm glad that those take longer to die away."

"Yeah, me too." He reached across the table and gave my hand a gentle squeeze. Just then, our food arrived.

"Wow! that was quick." I was shocked at how fast the service was. It was never that fast back at the pizza parlor. The waiter asked if we needed anything else and Sam sent him off.

"Well, on a brighter note, Danny, how are you liking Lancaster Farm?" He had a hopeful look in his eyes.

"Actually, it's been like a dream. I love it. It's hard

work, don't get me wrong, and I miss Henna, but it's hard to picture my life any other way. I could see staying here for a long time." I tried to exaggerate the last part. "You know, maybe I could get that business degree I'd been talking about and... I don't know... possibly we could run Lancaster Farm together." I looked at him hopefully.

He started to sweat a bit and pulled at his collar. "That's great. I'm glad to hear that." He blushed and it looked like he was reaching for his pocket. My breath hitched in my throat. *Was this it? Was this the moment?* My palms got sweaty and adrenaline flooded my veins. I stared at Sam in anticipation.

"I, er, I...," he started. "I wanted to ask you something." His face became pale with nerves.

"Yes?" I replied, expectantly.

"Um, well." He took his hand back out of his pocket empty and my heart sank. "How's the food?"

I couldn't even answer him. I knew I'd gotten my own hopes up, but I really needed him to finally admit his feelings for me. If he couldn't, then I couldn't stay. My heart was crushed. I loved him so much and I knew he had his own issues, but wasn't I worth it? *Am I not good enough for him to overcome his fears? Every moment we've spent together has been bliss. Why can't that be enough?* I wanted so badly for this man to fully be mine. He was already my safe space, my protector, maybe my one true love. But, I couldn't live a life on maybes.

Tears filled my eyes and I got up from the table and stormed toward the restaurant doors, leaving Sam's mouth agape behind me.

"Danny? Danny wait!" I could hear the realization in his voice that he'd upset me. It's high pitch told me he was scared. *He should be scared. He should be terrified of los-*

ing me.

I went all the way to the car, got in, and slammed the door. Silent tears fell down my face. Moments later Sam got in the driver's seat.

"What's wrong?" he ventured. He did sound truly concerned.

"Just take me home, Sam." My voice was barely a whisper. He didn't say any more as he put the car in drive.

∞ ∞ ∞

Sam had barely parked the car and I burst out the door. I took off the heels and ran into the house, tears still falling off my face. I headed straight for my room and slammed the door. I got out a duffle bag and started packing things into it.

I love him so much and he treats me so well. I caressed the necklace. *But, how long would I have to put my life on hold. I needed a commitment. I needed security in my life. I deserved to feel loved and never have to question it. If he can't prove it to me, then I can't stay.*

I was nearly packed up when Sam ventured into the room. My tears had subsided with my frantic packing. I zipped the bag shut. Sam stepped over to me. He touched my shoulder and my head snapped up. My accusatory eyes met his.

"Danny, stop," he begged. He must've figured what I was doing.

"Sam, if you can't even say 'I love you, Danny' then I can't stay. I think you know that. You said yourself 'As a horseman, you either conquer your fears or they conquer you.'" I was holding firm, but tears began to prick the backs of my eyes once more.

Sam ran a frantic hand through his hair, searching for the right words. "I know, I know. You deserve better than this, than me." He slunk down to sit on the bed. "I'm sorry I haven't told you, it's just... part of me wants you to leave." My eyes grew wide in shock and I froze. "To be honest, I'm just so afraid that you'll turn out exactly like Brittany. I know it's crazy and you're not her, but you have to understand that my mom passed away just after Brittany cheated on me. I was devastated. My heart couldn't take that again... So, even though I really don't want you to leave, I thought maybe if I held back just a little, you'd make that decision for me. But, now here you are making that choice. And here I am begging you not to go. Please... Danny." He stood up to take my hands. "I do love you."

My mouth fell open. I didn't know what to say.

He continued, "Danny, please, I truly do love you. I couldn't live if you weren't here. I need you. You need me. We fit together too perfectly for me to want to ever throw this away. Trust me."

"Sam, I do trust you."

"Then, give me one last chance to prove myself to you." Tears streaked down his face.

"Fine. One last chance."

Chapter 23

I threw on a tattered sweatshirt. The scent of coffee drifted up the stairs as Maxwell started the morning brew. Excitement bubbled in my veins. Things had been going so well since Sam finally started using the 'L' word. A wide smile spread across my face.

Spotting a pair of jeans by my bed, I started to shimmy into them. I lost my balance and stumbled into the side of my nightstand. Something fell to the floor. Thinking nothing of it, I continued to zip and then button my jeans when a familiar, blood-curdling sound came from the floor. My eyes shot downward and searched frantically, then I saw the screen of my phone light up a few steps away. Dropping to my hands and knees, I scrambled to turn it back off. The last thing I needed was for my phone to give away my location. My hands were shaking as I squeezed and held the top button to turn it off. The screen went dark. I carefully put it into the nightstand drawer. I trembled as I shut the drawer.

Just then, Sam burst into the room. "Hey, breakfast is ready!" He saw me sitting traumatized on the floor. "Danny, what's wrong?" He came to my aide.

"I... I dropped my phone. And it... it turned on." I hiccupped. "I think I shut it off in time, but I don't know. The screen lit up and it played its startup jingle. Then I squeezed the button and it went black, but," I looked up gravely at him, "what if it wasn't fast enough?"

He looked startled but puzzled on it for a moment before answering. "Well, you shut it off before it got to its home screen?"

"Yes."

"Okay. Then I seriously doubt that it had enough time to connect to any towers. Besides, the service out here is spotty at best. I don't think there's any cause for concern.

"I hope you're right." A shiver went down my spine.

"Try not to think about it. Besides, today is a day for having a little fun," he winked, "after we go do our chores. But first," Sam pointed his finger in the air, "breakfast!" He guided me out of the room. I looked back over my shoulder at the drawer.

Maxwell had prepared the typical spread on the table. The smell was heavenly. I felt a little nauseous from what had just occurred upstairs, but it didn't last. I poured myself a steaming cup of Joe and began to fill my plate. I noticed Max give Sam a strange look, but just brushed it off. Sam took up his usual spot and scooped a big pile of eggs onto his plate. I filled his coffee cup for him. He buttered us some bread. Breakfast disappeared fast.

We were sitting at the table, finished with our food, and sipping on the remnants of our coffee. Sam broke the silence.

"Danny, I was hoping you'd be interested in going on a longer trail ride with me today. I know a really nice spot way out back. If you're up for it."

"Yeah, that sounds like fun. Just a day trip?"

"Yeah, if we blaze through morning chores and set off right after, we could be back for dinner. We'd just pack a lunch."

"Sounds like a fun plan to me!" I got a little excited for some much-needed alone time with Sam.

"Great!" Sam grinned. "And Dad already volunteered to muck out the stalls for us!" Sam beamed at Maxwell.

"Wow! Thanks, Max!" I said.

"My pleasure." Max gave me an unusually warm grin, then he looked back at Sam. They stared at each other for a moment before Sam got up from the table.

"Well, it's about time to get at it then." He set his coffee cup in the sink. "Danny, why don't you take the nursery barn and feed, and I'll take some horses out to pasture. Then, we can get Charlie and Clarabelle ready to go."

"Alrighty." I smirked.

Once we got outside, we all went our separate ways. I made my way over to the nursery barn. Shoving the door open, I flipped on the lights. I saw several horses and a bunch of smaller faces staring back at me. The foals from the spring were already getting tall, but they were still cute. I got to work in the first pen.

Opening the stall door, I gently pushed the tall foal back, away from the entrance. As I grabbed the water bucket, it stuck its head over my shoulder. Little whiskers tickled my ear.

"Hey, get out of my ear, buddy." I giggled at how nosey the young ones were. I stood up and the he followed me to the door. I was careful to keep him in the pen while I snuck out and dumped the dirty water outside. I returned the empty bucket to the stall, gave the foal and momma both a kiss on their soft, velvety noses, and shut the stall door. Then, I dumped out the next stall's water bucket and then the next, battling the curiosity of the adorable young ones as I went. Next, I grabbed the water hose from the wall and turned on the faucet. I dragged the hose out a little way, so I'd have ample room to fill the buckets. Sticking the hose through the rungs in the stall, I filled each bucket. The water was ice cold as it gently back splashed onto me. My hands lithely recoiled the hose and then grabbed the pocketknife in the window-sill. The knife glided through the strings on the hay bale with ease. Returning the knife back to the sill, I grabbed the bale twine and set it in the twine bucket. Then, I took flakes of hay, reached up, and squished them in the top part of the feeders in each stall.

Finally, I prepared buckets of grain for each feeder. Some oats, some pellets, and a dash of molasses for pal-atability. I took a deep breath in as it smelled heavenly; sweet with a hint of musk, earth, and vanilla. Each stall got its grain ration, and all of the horses were munching away as I did one last check through the stalls. All seemed to be in order, so I turned out the lights and shut the door.

It was a crisp, late fall day. I shuddered in my sweat-shirt. Sam was taking some horses out to pasture. I picked the remnants of hay out of my hair as I made my way over to the main barn. Maxwell popped out of the barn doors with a wheelbarrow full of muck. He smiled as he passed me by. Entering the dim lit barn, I saw that Sam had nearly finished taking horses out, so I grabbed Clarabelle's halter and lead.

Walking to Clarabelle's stall, I slid open the steel door. She was waiting calmly inside and perked up as she saw me. Her ears flicked forward; her interest piqued. I strode in, whispering sweet nothings to her as I slid the halter over her soft nose and her fuzzy ears. My fingers nimbly clipped the lead rope on the halter and I led her out of the stall. I brought her to stand and hooked the cross ties to each side of her halter. Then, I retrieved Charlie from his stall and hooked him to the other set of ties. Using a stiff-bristled, wooden brush, I got to work getting the dust off of them. I then picked their hooves of debris and gave them a once over to make sure all was well.

Next, I collected the saddle and heaved it onto Clarabelle's back. My nerves started to tingle a little as I became excited over our day trip. I found Sam's saddle and set it onto Charlie's back, then pulled up the cinches on my saddle and grabbed the bridle. The bit made tinkling sounds like wind chimes. I loved the way the old leather smelled too; a little musky, a little sweet. Plus, the equipment smelled like horses and I was learning to love that scent very much.

Sam walked in as I had just finished slipping the bridle on Clarabelle. I was giving her velvety nose kisses and muttering to her. He walked up behind me and slipped his arms around me. My body warmed in his embrace and his lips sent little kisses down the back of my neck. My hair stood on end as I tingled with pleasure. Sam spun me around and pressed his lips strongly to mine, nearly taking my breath away. I pushed him away slightly.

"Someone is excited about our trip."

Sam smirked. "You've got that right." I grinned in return. He glanced over the horses. "Hey, you have my saddle out. Thanks!"

"No problem. You said you wanted to shove off as soon as possible, so I have Clarabelle ready too."

"Nice. I'll finish up with Charlie then. Why don't you grab us some other supplies? How about something to snack on for lunch and some water?" Sam's eyes turned mischievous. "And maybe a blanket or two?" He winked.

I rolled my eyes. "Okay. I'll get on that." I strode past him and he gave me a playful pat on my rear. My head snapped back over my shoulder, so I could stick my tongue out at him.

Before long, we were all packed and ready to go. The horses were stomping their feet with anticipation and I was feeling the same. I was sitting on Clarabelle, waiting for Sam to be done conversing with Maxwell before we shoved off. He was taking unusually long. Finally, Max patted Sam on the shoulder and he jogged over to us and climbed aboard Charlie. Sam led the way down the dusty trail toward the back of the Lancaster estate.

The horses' hooves clipped and clopped along the gravel path. A chill breeze rustled the leaves gathered against the pasture fences. Horses were calmly grazing what was left of the pastures in the mid-morning sun. We continued on and broke free of paddocks and fences and passed the dirt track. Sam was leading us around the hill we normally climbed to get into the woods. Instead, he took us down a different path. As we skirted the first hills, Sam quietly followed an overgrown trail that divided two large fields.

The wind whirled through the tall grass, creating a subtle rustle. My mind pondered where we might be headed. There were patches of forest in the distance and a very tall hill, almost a mountain, standing in the center. From what I could make out, it was mostly covered in trees, but also had some rocky terrain. I gently squeezed my legs together to encourage Clarabelle to go faster. We fell into stride with Charlie and Sam.

I didn't have one of my own, but Sam was wearing his dark brown cowboy hat. His tousled brown hair fell down a little passed his ears. He was dressed rather sharply for a casual trail ride. He wore a long-sleeve button-down shirt paired with a fancy pair of dark blue jeans. His shirt even had intricate tribal designs and a complex yolk. It looked like one of Amanda's show shirts from when she used to ride in competitions. Then, there was me in my everyday duds.

"So, will you tell me now where we're going?" I inquired.

"Nope," Sam replied, simply. "It's a surprise."

"Ugh. Okay." I still felt like that rascal was up to something.

I allowed Clarabelle to fall back in line behind Charlie. My mind reeled as I tried to guess our destination. *Somewhere in the field? Into the woods? Would I have to scale that mountain?*

All I knew for sure is that he said it would be a daytrip. We would be home around supper time. That made the mountain the most likely candidate. My stomach did a little flip just thinking about taking one wrong step on the steep side. My old apartment building was tall, but there were elevators. Heights still gave me the willies. Besides, it seemed to me to be tough enough to climb that tiny hill on our regular trail on horseback. There's a lot of mechanics that go into riding on inclines and declines and varying terrain. I didn't know if I was ready for such a challenge. Leave it to Sam to demand the best from me.

My nerves tingled even more as Sam began to lead us directly in the mountain's path. As we continued, the fields gave way to patchy grasslands. Bushes and shrubs shot up here and there. Rocks dotted the landscape, some as large as a car. As the mountain loomed closer, deciduous trees dwindled, and coniferous pines took their place. Their dark green shone starkly against the limestone base of the mountain. Sam led us towards the bottom, where I could just make out the remnants of a trail.

It was clear that no one had been this way for a long time, but I didn't blame them. It looked like a complex journey. A thought crossed my mind. *Did the Lancasters' really own all of this? All the way out here?*

Sam halted and hopped off Charlie. I pulled up on Clarabelle and carefully swung my legs over her rump and slid down. "Sam does your family really own all of this?"

Sam strode around Charlie's backside and wrapped an arm around my shoulders while he admired the mountain. "Well, we've been farming for generations, not always horses. My great grandfather was a cattle rancher and he ran his cattle on this land. You need a lot of pasture and grazing land when you let cows' free range. So, to answer your question, yes."

"Wow. And someday, all of this shall be yours," I joked.

"Yeah... just mine." Sam smirked and blushed a little. He rubbed a hand on his neck suspiciously.

"What?"

"Oh, nothing." He grinned and pressed a sweet kiss against my unexpecting lips. My heart fluttered.

Regathering myself, I exclaimed, "What was that for?"

"I just love you, that's all."

"Awe, you're so sweet." I gave him a playful punch in the arm, then grazed a soft kiss upon his stubbly cheek. We looked back up at the mountain.

"Are you nervous?" Sam asked.

"Insanely."

"Good. You probably should be." *Wow, how comforting.* "And I know you've never done anything quite this advanced, so I've got some pointers." Sam looked me dead in the eyes. "And if at any time you feel you can't do it, or it gets to challenging, just lemme know, okay? I can always hop on Clarabelle or we can hike up, too. However, I know both of these horses are veterans of this trail."

"Okay. I'll let you know if I can't handle it, but don't think I'll give up that easily. You've taught me better than that." I surprised myself at my newfound determination. Thanks to Sam, I was always trying to be better and challenge myself. I was doing things every day that I would've thought were impossible. His fire only served to fuel mine. Heck, he's the one that ignited mine. "So, what're my pointers?" I eagerly craved to prove my worth on these trails.

Sam gave me a smirk. He must have seen the flames dancing in my eyes. "Well, it's similar to our other trails, but it's more rocky and in some areas, steep. So, you'll wanna be extra cautious and stay on your toes. We'll also have a river to cross, deeper than what you've done before. And as a reminder, lean back and push your stirrups forward going downhill, turn your horse's head downhill when turning on the hillside, and lean forward and give Clara her head when going uphill."

"Got it. Let's go!" I marched my way back toward Clarabelle.

Sam came scrambling after me. "Slow down there speed racer. Lemme check your saddle fit. Safety first. It's important."

"Thanks, baby. Always looking out for me." I obnoxiously batted my eyelashes at him.

Sam finished checking and adjusting our saddles. "Ready?" His eyebrows were raised under his cowboy hat.

"Ready," I replied, and we mounted back up.

Sam began to lead the way again. Limestone gravel crunched under hoof as we started the ascent. Under some tree cover, it got even cooler and I shuddered. So far, the trail was decent, just rocky. I had to be extra aware of where I told Clarabelle to go. However, watching Sam's muscular frame, from his broad shoulders down to his swaying hips, was a bit distracting.

I peered down through an opening in the trees to see we had made it about a third of the way up. Bringing my eyes back to the trail, I could see we were at the start of a sharp incline. A jolt of adrenaline shot through my veins. My palms got a little clammy, but I was determined to make Sam proud. I gritted my teeth and took a breath. Charlie grunted with effort as he began to climb. Then, Clara huffed as we started. I felt her muscles work under me and I gave her more reins as I leaned forward into the grade. Rocks tumbled away behind us and my nerves fluttered once more. I kept my eyes pinned forward, right between her ears. The steep grade tapered level again as the path curved against the hillside. Clarabelle shook her head defiantly as we returned to the flatter path.

The path zigzagged up the mountainside. We made it through an incline, a flat, and another jolt upwards. Then, we were on another flat spot as I heard the babbling of water. Soon, the river Sam had mentioned came into view. He took Charlie right into it, without hesitation. I brought Clara to a halt at the edge as I watched them cross. It was not much more than a horse-length wide, but my heart lurched as I saw the water lap up to Charlie's chest. Sam didn't bother picking up his legs, he just let them dangle in the water. It would be cool at this time of the year. Clarabelle sensed my apprehension as her feet began to dance under me. However, within a minute, Sam had made it back up the bank on the other side. He turned Charlie to face me.

"C'mon. You can do this!" he called to me.

I peered down the river and watched as its fast current flowed down the mountain and out of sight. My stomach turned in knots. I squeezed my eyes shut.

"Danny, you've got this. You've made it this far already! You're doing awesome. You'll be fine, I promise. Trust Clarabelle to get you through. It'll all be worth it, trust me. We're almost to the top." I let Sam's calming voice ease my mind.

Forcing my eyes open, I drove Clara onward. We plunged into the river and I stifled a yelp from the water's icy fingertips. The water lapped at Clarabelle's midchest. She pushed on and we crawled, dripping, up the other bank. A big smile broke across Sam's face and mine too.

"Told ya you could do it," Sam declared. He didn't even wait for my response, he just turned Charlie and continued on toward another sharp incline. I shivered from my wet legs. We continued following the river upward and finally, we crested the summit. I had to lean back and push my stirrups forward to balance out while making a sharp descent. We turned and made it to a plateau in the opposite side of the mountain. Sam was certainly right. It was totally worth the trip. Sam dismounted and came to give me a hand off my horse. It felt good to stand on my own two legs again.

"Well? What do you think? Go ahead and check it out," Sam grinned and motioned toward our surroundings.

I took his encouragement and surveyed the area. It was breathtaking. The river we had followed on the other side was only a portion of the river that cascaded down this side. We were standing on a precipice of sorts, with a pool of water, created from the many years of a gorgeous waterfall tumbling into it. I approached the ledge and peered over. The river continued out of the pool in a little stream which flowed right over the edge. The spray from the little fall created a rainbow below me as the sun glinted off the water. It was beautiful set against the backdrop of great pine trees. Rolling hills and smaller mountains went on for miles. A myriad of vegetation covered the landscape. A hundred shades of green and tan, all set against the bright blue backdrop of the early afternoon sky. The subtle sounds of the cascading waterfalls made it flawless.

I was soaking it all in when Sam's voice startled me. The crashing of the falls had masked his approach. "Danny, I have a question for you." His voice wavered a bit.

I turned to face him, and my heart stopped. The air left my lungs and my mouth turned to cotton. My eyes widened, cheeks flushed, and palms became clammy. I thought I might pass out and fall off the edge. Sam's suspicious activities all began to make sense.

Here before me was a man, more breathtaking to me than the landscape beside us, down on one knee. A small box was open in his hands. It held a small diamond ring, sterling silver, with intricate filigree accents. My eyes welled up and I put a hand over my gaping mouth.

"Danny, I know I've had some trouble with my feelings in the past." He giggled a bit. "I actually tried asking you this same question when I took you out to dinner about a month ago. I'm so sorry my fears got the better of me. But I've never been more sure of anything." He looked deeply into my eyes. "Will you do me the honor of becoming my wife?" Sam's eyes shone bright and hopeful. As if there was ever a chance that I would say no.

"Yes!" I shrieked. Tears rolled down my cheeks as I

dove into his arms. He barely had time to stand up. He pressed me hard against his chest. Then, gently, he grabbed my hand to slip my new ring on my finger. It was perfect. All of it. He turned my face away from my hand and back up to his. His hazel eyes burned into mine.

"I love you," he said simply. It was a pure sentence. Music to my ears. It's all I ever wanted to hear. That someone loved me, the way that he did.

"I love you, too." I replied. In that moment, we just gazed into each other's souls. I found my hero, my knight in shining armor, my future, my destiny, all rolled into a perfect package.

I could feel the electricity sparking between us. Our souls were colliding on some deep spiritual level we could never begin to comprehend. Sam's powerful arm pulled me in tightly and he kissed me fiercely. It was a cold day, but I could feel the heat. I wrapped my arms around his neck, feeling his strength as he scooped me into his arms with ease. He carried me toward the waterfall and we slipped behind it, entering a small cave. Sam had already laid out our picnic blanket, but we were much too preoccupied for food. He set me down gently and we began to tear off each other's clothes. I saved his cowboy hat for last as I admired his form and then gave it a flick off with my hand. Sam guided me down to the blanket. I ran my fingertips over his mighty body. It was like touching Hercules. He kissed me everywhere his lips could reach as the spray from the waterfall sent chills down my spine. As the water crashed into the pool and became one, we did, too — our bodies and souls colliding in euphoria.

Chapter 24

As we packed up after our late lunch, I couldn't stop staring at my hand. Looking at the glittering diamond entranced me into a state of disbelief. *How could I go from living every day in fear for my life, to living everyday like it was a perfect gift from God, or the universe itself? Could it get any better than this?* I looked over at Sam carefully packing the blankets into the saddle bag. Then, I glanced around the scenic view once more. *This is peak perfection.* I brought the rest of the remnants from lunch over to Sam.

"I'll have to grumble at Maxwell! I saw you dirty dogs talking this morning. Man, everyone knew about it, except me," I joked.

Sam rechecked Clarabelle's girth. "Well, that *was* the goal. You were surprised, weren't you?"

I rolled my eyes as Sam helped me back onto Clara. "Sam, I nearly fell off the cliff in shock."

He grinned from ear to ear. "I know. It was truly priceless." He hauled himself onto Charlie's back, then came to stand side by side with Clarabelle and me. His eyes met mine. They twinkled with pride and it warmed my heart. The way he looked at me made me feel like a queen, like I was truly worth something; a feeling he'd given me since the beginning. Something I had never quite known before.

He leaned in towards me. I smirked and leaned in too,

nearly colliding with the brim of his cowboy hat. I lifted it up a little, so I could sneak under. Our lips locked. My mind was blank, save for the sound of the waterfall. My worldly worries melted away. I drew back and just looked at him in amazement, admiring the immaculate work of art in front of me, from his hat to his boots. I felt like I could stare at him forever and I would still run out of time.

"Shall we head back home and share the good news?" Sam interrupted my musing.

I looked at the trail and up at the sky. The sun was on its way down toward the horizon and ominous clouds were beginning to move in. Although I could've stayed in that moment infinitely, it looked like a storm was brewing.

"Yes, let's start our trek back." Sam, naturally, took the lead. We headed back up the trail toward the opposite side of the mountain. We crested the top and I took one last glance at the picturesque view behind me, reminiscing on the wild ride the day had been. Wild, but wonderful. I couldn't wait to tell Maxwell when we got home.

The return journey was a bit more treacherous than journey up the mountain. Clarabelle was almost skidding down the gravel at times, it was so steep. Loose rocks tumbling down in front of us. It made me uneasy. Thankfully, she was pretty sure footed. I just needed to put my faith in her and we made it successfully to the bottom.

Once we were on flat land again, I became lackadaisical and let Clara take most of the control. My mind was wandering back to the waterfall, the gentle spray of the water and Sam's body against mine. I glanced down once more at the ring on my finger. I felt like a fairytale princess about to marry her prince charming and live happily ever after. It sounded ridiculous in my head and quite unbelievable that my life could ever turn out this way. I never thought I'd be happy, not truly anyway.

I'm glad Clarabelle was nearly broke to death because I hadn't been paying attention at all. Sam had led us nearly back to the paddocks. It would be nice to get off Clarabelle. My legs were getting sore from riding most of the day and I could tell she was exhausted, too. It had been a long trek for the horses since they don't climb mountains like that every day. But I was glad they were such supportive, faithful companions. Horses are one-of-a-kind creatures.

I was admiring Vera and Lightning as we passed their paddock when, suddenly, I heard shouting toward the farmhouse. It sounded like Maxwell. And another voice too, but I could barely make it out. Sam looked back at me, worry in his eyes, and without speaking, we both urged our horses to run.

Wind whipping through my hair, we sped towards the house. Once we reached the barn, my blood curdled. Sheer terror gripped me like an invisible hand. It felt like the air was being sucked from my lungs.

Maxwell was on the steps of the front porch, his hands in the air and none other than my father, Bill, was pointing a pistol straight at him. I started to panic, but we didn't stop running. Finally, we reached the house and jumped off our horses, about 15 feet away from the scene. Maxwell looked over at us, panic in his eyes, too. Bill followed his gaze and whipped around, pistol following.

Sam immediately stepped in front of me. I peered around his shoulder.

"Out of the way, boy!" Bill shouted angrily. "Danny,

you better come with me," he slurred. He was clearly drunk. And furious. Not a good combination. The old horrors that plagued my life all came flooding back to me. I trembled.

"She's not going anywhere," Sam declared defiantly.

"She's my daughter! You have no say in this matter! Now get out of my way!"

"She's not going anywhere with you. Put the gun down. We can settle this rationally," Sam demanded, as calmly as he could.

Bill staggered a few steps forward. "I am being rational, you took her away from me. She belongs to me. Out of my way!" Bill shouted, stumbling a bit closer. Sam tensed.

Sam took a few steps forward as he tried to explain. "We didn't take her from you. Danny ran away from home. She found us, and we took her in." His voice was beginning to waver.

"Liar!" Bill roared in anger and the pistol that was pointed at Sam went off.

"Sam!" I shrieked in horror. For a few seconds, I stood there hyperventilating. *What are we going to do?* Frozen to the spot, I glanced over at Maxwell who had slowly crept his way to the door of the house. My mind reeled. Maxwell needed a good enough distraction to get inside with that creaky house door. I knew what I needed to. I sent up a prayer for all of us, looked down at Sam's motionless body, blood already staining the ground, and then looked back up at Bill.

Hatred began to replace my fear. I let out a furious battle cry and rushed forward. Letting my emotions fuel me, I lunged for the pistol gripped in his hand. Out of the corner of my eye, I caught Maxwell running into the house. I just needed to buy him some time.

Bill and I wrestled for the gun. It was swinging this way and that. If only I could pry his fingers off of it. I used all of the force I had to keep the gun facing away from myself, while still maintaining my grip. This insane man didn't even realize he could have easily shot and killed his own daughter with his own stupidity. Seconds began to feel like hours and my stamina was beginning to wane. Bill was so much bigger than I was, so much stronger. As we stumbled around, wrestling for the gun, it began to rain. The metal of the pistol became slick. Sweat was running down the back of my neck. I needed to make a move and fast, or someone else was going to get hurt.

I struggled to get my finger to the trigger, but I made it in behind the trigger guard and kept it there, waiting for my opportunity. The gun swung up and down between us. I took my chance and shoved the gun in toward Bill, pulling the trigger. BANG!

Bill stopped struggling and looked me dead in the eyes for a second. I looked back but felt no mercy. I let him slump to the ground, gun still gripped in my fingers. Rain poured as blood spilled from his wound. He looked up at the sky as his eyes clouded over. I popped out the ammunition and let it fall along with the pistol. Thunder clapped overhead as lightning flashed across the sky.

Maxwell ran passed me. I whipped around and saw Sam still lying motionless, now with a pool of blood around him. I ran over, hot tears streaking down my face. Maxwell and I knelt down beside him. Sam had been shot in the left shoulder area. It was too hard to tell if it would've hit any vital organs, but he was bleeding badly. Maxwell checked his pulse. Relief flashed across his face as tears welled in his eyes.

"He has a pulse," he said, shakily. "I called the police. They're sending an ambulance. They should be here any minute. Here, use this towel to put on some pressure."

"Okay," it was all I could muster to say. I pushed down on the towel. Maxwell got up and went over to check Bill's pulse too. I glanced over, already knowing the answer as Maxwell just shook his head. Maxwell came back over to us and knelt back down beside Sam. My eyes fell back upon my father's lifeless body. I had no remorse, only disgust. Angry tears rolled down my already drenched face and I looked back down at Sam. *Just when I thought we could be happy. Don't you dare leave me now!*

The sirens blared in the distance. Relief flooded my veins as the ambulance and police cars pulled in. I kept pressure on Sam's wound until the EMS came and took over. They pushed me aside and I stood, shaking, next to Maxwell. He put an arm around me and drew me in close. I sobbed into his chest as they carried Sam into the ambulance. Then, the police came over to question us. Maxwell did most of the talking as I could barely get a peep out without hyperventilating.

The crime scene investigators began to examine the scene and take pictures of Bill's prone form. By that time, Maxwell and I were soaked from head to toe in the rain and I could no longer tell if I was shivering from the events or from the cold. The police told us there would be more questioning, but for the time being, we were not being held. Maxwell led me into the house.

"Go get changed and we'll head to the hospital," Maxwell instructed. "I'll bring Charlie and Clarabelle in and change, too."

I just nodded. My mind and body were numb as I walked up the stairs. As I stood in my bedroom shivering, water dripped off of me and onto the floor. Looking down at the ring on my hand, I started sobbing, dropping to my knees.

Maxwell must have heard me because, after he changed, he slowly came into my room. I was still on the floor, sniffling. He knelt down on the floor and wrapped a warm towel around me, holding me for a moment.

"It's gonna be okay." He started rocking me gently back and forth. "You need to just breathe. In and out. Slowly. Can you do that for me?" His deep, smooth voice was calming.

I nodded and tried to get my breathing under control. Maxwell gave me a few minutes to just breathe, then he stood up.

"Okay. Let's get you up." He gave me a hand. "Sit on the bed and I'll find something warm in your closet. I plopped down on the edge of the bed while Maxwell went to search in my closet. Watching him, I knew exactly where Sam got his sweet and doting disposition from. I would be proud to call this man family.

Maxwell returned with a big, comfy sweatshirt and sweatpants. He instructed me to put them on. He stepped out for a moment while I peeled out of my drenched clothes and slipped into the dry ones. Then, he popped back in with a brush and a hair tie. He had me sit on the edge of the bed while he combed through my wet, tangled hair and put it up in a pony for me.

"There. Beautiful." Maxwell gave me a squeeze around my shoulders. "Now, let's go see our boy."

Chapter 25

I didn't sleep a wink that night. I stayed up holding Sam's hand and watching his monitor. The doctors had told us that the bullet had missed his lungs by inches and that, in time, he would be good as new. It was music to our ears. Henna had been sitting with me since midnight and Amanda showed up early in the morning and sat with Maxwell in the waiting area. We were all waiting eagerly for Sam to wake up.

Finally, around mid-morning, he opened his eyes. My heart flooded with joy as I saw his gorgeous hazel eyes looking back at me.

"Sam! You're awake! How are you feeling?" I asked quietly. Henna slipped out of the room to get the others.

Sam looked down at his arm in a cast and sling. "Um, I'm okay, I guess. Groggy. The last thing I remember is the gun going off and I thought I was a goner."

A tear rolled down my cheek. "We thought you were gonna be a goner too, for a bit. The doctors said the bullet missed your lungs by mere inches. I was terrified..."

Sam sat up more and used his good hand to wipe away my tears. "You can't get rid of me that easily." He smirked and reached for my hand. He glanced at the ring. "That looks so good on you." Sam's eyes twinkled. He pulled me in for a quick kiss.

Just then, everyone came into the room and fussed over Sam. Amanda gave him a big kiss on the cheek.

I faded to the background and just admired all of the people in the room. They were all the family I had now, but they were all I ever needed.

That afternoon, they released Sam from the hospital and we drove home. It was relatively quiet during the ride; we were all so tired. When we pulled into the familiar drive, I saw that Mark had started doing barn chores. As much as I had gotten a bad vibe from him before, he was doing his part to help out in our time of need.

Maxwell parked the car and I got out. I went around the other side of the car to open Sam's door for him.

"Hm, this is a bit of a role reversal," he said, stepping out of the car. Even after all of the insanity that had passed, he was still cracking jokes.

"Yeah, yeah. Let's get you inside, shall we?"

Maxwell held the door for us as we went up the stairs. Amanda pulled in the driveway with her car and she stepped out with an armload of fast food.

"Hey! Alright! Thanks, Sis!" Sam called to her.

"Wow. Do I know you or what?" Amanda grinned, showing off the bag like a trophy.

We headed inside and all grabbed a bite to eat. I sat next to Sam in my usual spot and munched away hungrily. I surprised myself with how hungry I was. However, I hadn't eaten anything since lunch the day before. I wolfed down my food quickly and tossed my garbage in the trash.

"I'm gonna go help Mark finish chores," I called out as I headed for the door.

"Danny, no, let me. You don't have to do that," Amanda said.

"Oh, don't worry about it. I'm glad to." I walked out the door. Truth was, I was happy to have a moment of distraction and some quiet time with the horses. Coming down the steps, I looked over at where my father's body had been. Blood stained the dead grass and leaves. It sent a shiver down my spine, and as horrible as it sounded, I was glad to be rid of him. There was no chance of him ever coming back to hurt us and, for that, I was thankful.

I walked into the main barn and found Mark filling the waters in each stall.

"Hi, Mark. How far did you get?" To my surprise, he greeted me with a much kinder disposition than last time.

"Hey, I'm so sorry about what happened. I have all of the grain and hay in the stalls waiting for the horses. Amanda told me what to do. I'm working on water, and have a few more to go."

"Wow, thanks. I'll go get the horses then." He gave me a curt nod and I grabbed two lead ropes and headed for the door.

I made quick work of gathering the horses and used the time to clear my mind. I saved Vera and Lightning for last since I had a special affinity for them. The young horses were getting bigger and bigger by the day. I walked into their paddock and called out to them. I heard the thunder of their hooves as they both came running toward me. Vera whickered softly as she approached, then touched her muzzle to my cheek.

I smiled. Her warm breath caressed my skin. "Hey, you goon," I said to her quietly. Giving her a kiss on the nose, I clipped on the lead. Lightning was nuzzling my back pocket, hoping to find some apple treats that I usually stashed there. Clipping the lead on him too, we walked out of the paddock. The horses' hoofbeats calmed my nerves; their musky, sweet scent was equally as soothing. I watched as their heads swayed side to side, walking alongside me. This was a sight that I was very glad I'd get to see for the rest of my life. Mark was waiting at the big barn door to close it behind us as we went passed him.

"I'm heading in then!" he called to me.

"Okay, sounds good! Thanks again!"

"No problem!" he said, closing the big door.

I unclipped Vera and Lightning, and watched as they went right to their respective stalls and walked in.

"Good job, guys!" I praised as I shut the doors behind them.

I walked to the front of the barn and opened the door. I flicked off the lights and just stood in the doorway for a moment, listening to the sounds of the horses munching away on their hay and grain. It was like a song in life I never knew I needed to hear. I stepped out, closed the door behind me, and made my way to the house. The lights shone out of the windows and onto the ground as the daylight waned. The sun was sinking low in the sky, creating a crimson skyline.

Coming up the steps of the porch, I found Sam sitting on the swing, apparently waiting for me. Approaching him, I found he had two cups of hot cocoa, one in his hand and the other on the seat next to him. I snatched it up and plunked down on the swing. We turned our gaze to the sunset.

"Thank you, Sam. It's perfect."

"Of course, my dear. Anything for you."

"You really do mean that, don't you? I mean, you stepped right in front of me without hesitation."

"And I'd do it over and over again," Sam replied plainly.

"I know you would." I leaned over and kissed him on the cheek.

"So, what happens now?" he asked. "Will there be a trial?"

"Yes. Maxwell already got an attorney for me. He said that my case looks good for self-defense. That it meets all of the criteria required. So, I should be exonerated."

"Good. I'm glad. I didn't really want to have a jailhouse wedding." He grinned down at me.

"Oh, my God. You're jokes are terrible. You know that right?"

"Well, of course I know that. But, you love me for it. You know you do."

"Sure." I rolled my eyes.

"Speaking of wedding planning, I think Amanda is gonna explode. She's trying to hold it back, in light of these events, but since she's known the longest that I was gonna ask you, she has, like, a whole binder prepared already. So, consider yourself fair warned."

"Oh, boy. Great. Well, at least she's excited. That makes at least two of us." I looked down giddily at my ring.

"You're excited, too? Hmm, I couldn't tell. I mean, it's not like you nearly dove into my arms on the mountain or anything."

I stuck my tongue out at him. He squeezed me around the shoulders with his good arm. I cuddled in close as the temperature dropped as the sun sank below the horizon. I took a sip of my hot cocoa.

Sam broke the silence. "I can't wait to spend the rest of my life with you and grow old together. Do you think we'll still sit out here, like this, in fifty years?"

"I think so. I mean, we'll have a whole yard full of grandkids by then I suppose, but yes. Much like this." I looked out over the yard and beyond at all of what would someday be ours.

"You sure know how to paint a pretty picture. That sounds perfect to me." My gaze returned to Sam. His hazel eyes were bright as he was looking deeply at me. He leaned in and kissed me sweetly.

A breeze rolled through and I snuggled in closer to him, a cup of warm cocoa in my hands. The yard light turned on as the last remnants of the sun were fading away. Crickets were chirping in the background. Sam's body heat and scent enveloped me. The low mumblings and laughter of Maxwell, Mark, and Amanda were coming from inside. Even in times of chaos, this family stuck together and never lost hope. They were the best people I'd ever met, and I was so glad to be able to soon call them my real family.

I finally found where I truly belonged, safe and loved. After all these years of torture since my mother passed, I thought nothing would ever be right in my world again. I could barely fathom all of the anguish I went through. Sometimes, all it takes to fix your life is to just take a chance. My leap of faith actually worked. Fate, destiny, or divine intervention brought us together. Looking out, I could see my forever and I wouldn't have it any other way.

About The Author

Casey L Brown

Casey is an instructor of Canine Psychology and Obedience, an entrepreneur, and an Amazon best-selling author.

She is the owner of a pet sitting and dog training business. Casey writes in both the nonfiction and fiction worlds with books in dog training and obedience and young adult romance.

Casey is certified in Canine Psychology and Obedience. She has a Bachelor degree in Business Management as well as three Associate degrees in Dairy Science, Agri-business, and Crop Science.

Since middle school, Casey has loved writing and began work on her first book in the seventh grade. Currently, she enjoys writing fiction and helping others with her dog behavior and training books. Her other interests in-

clude; reading, training her miniature horse and donkey on the family farm, and spending time with her husband and family.

To find out more about Casey, please visit her website at https://www.clbrownauthor.com/

www.ingramcontent.com/pod-product-compliance
Lightning Source LLC
Chambersburg PA
CBHW021040130626
46552CB00005B/1935